Urgent Fury

The Ranger Creed

R Recognizing that I volunteered as a Ranger, fully knowing the hazards of my chosen profession, I will always endeavor to uphold the prestige, honor, and high esprit de corps of my Ranger Regiment.

A Acknowledging the fact that a Ranger is a more elite soldier who arrives at the cutting edge of battle by land, sea, or air, I accept the fact that as a Ranger my country expects me to move further, faster and fight harder than any other soldier.

N Never shall I fail my comrades. I will always keep myself mentally alert, physically strong and morally straight and I will shoulder more than my share of the task whatever it may be, one-hundred-percent and then some.

G Gallantly will I show the world that I am a specially selected and well-trained soldier. My courtesy to superior officers, neatness of dress and care of equipment shall set the example for others to follow.

E Energetically will I meet the enemies of my country. I shall defeat them on the field of battle for I am better trained and will fight with all my might. Surrender is not a Ranger word. I will never leave a fallen comrade to fall into the hands of the enemy and under no circumstances will I ever embarrass my country.

R Readily will I display the intestinal fortitude required to fight on to the Ranger objective and complete the mission though I be the lone survivor.

Rangers Lead The Way!!!

Written by Command Sergeant Major Neal R. Gentry, 1974

The Archive Obscura *presents*

Urgent Fury

Parachute assaults, hostage rescues,
and America's first contact
with an ancient evil.

Washington, D.C.

The Archive Obscura
www.archiveobscura.com
@thearchiveobscura

ISBN 979-8-218-30448-5
LCCN 2023948689

This is a work of fiction. References to actual people, places, organizations, and events are intended for entertainment purposes only. References to government organizations do not constitute endorsement of any kind.

This does not contain classified material. All historical information used is in the public domain and collected outside of government classification systems and protocols.

No disrespect intended. This story is a fictionalized account of a real conflict that left lasting physical, emotional, and spiritual repercussions for both combatants and civilians alike. No part of this story is meant to trivialize the experiences of those affected by the conflict.

Cover Photo Credit: SGT Praxedis Pineda / dvidshub.net

This page left blank intentionally

The Archive Obscura
of the United States

To whom it may concern,

The Archive Obscura has worked in the shadows since 1947, the first year the government needed to quickly collect, catalog, and store artifacts and documentation of a paranormal nature. President Truman secretly founded our organization on two principles: 1) any unexplained persons, technology, or event could pose a serious security threat to the United States until proven otherwise, and 2) the great paradigm shifts that the "unexplainable" often represent can undercut societal foundations such as science, religion, and commerce. For these reasons, any and all unexplained discoveries default to the strictest classification standard and come under the purview of our collection.

My staff and I were taken aback when we learned that the secrets we had been custodians of for so long would now be subject to the Freedom of Information Act (FOIA) and compelled declassification procedures. Our personal opinions aside, we serve at the behest of our citizenry and the chosen elected leaders. As such, we will execute our duties to disclose these files in their entirety as instructed.

We have prepared the subsequent version for the public's examination. Documents have been scanned in the same order as they appear in the file. Since this is an internal government report, there is a significant amount of jargon. I have had my staff include footnotes and other helpful notations to assist in understanding the full context.

As you read through this summary prepared for then-President Reagan, please keep in mind that only a year passed since the incident. The 1980s was a time limited in investigatory and scientific means relative to today's advancements. Those responding were certainly not equipped to manage such a unique incident.

Very few can recall *Operation Urgent Fury* today. It was quickly overshadowed by the invasion of Panama a few years later, and then by the neverending series of police actions of the 1990s. By the time the United States was fully engrossed in the Global War on Terror in the 2000s, what happened in Grenada in 1983 was fully erased from the public consciousness.

As the following declassified documents will show, the military stumbled across something truly sinister those two days in October. Political strife and corporate greed combined to incubate a supernatural contagion. The world was fortunate to have the Army Rangers there as they were uniquely suited to combating the violent infestation.

In my opinion, they may have saved the world.

The Curator

Washington D.C.

This page left blank intentionally

Final Report on Operation Urgent Fury Paranormal Incident
FILE CONTENTS

SECTION ONE - BACKGROUND

The following section presents evidence collected before the October 1983 incident. It provides all the contextual information available to decision makers prior to the invasion. It also highlights the key decisions that likely instigated the incident.

INTRODUCTION

Central Intelligence Agency
Office of the Inspector General (OIG)
Langley, VA

October 1984

Memorandum For: President of the United States (POTUS), Ronald Reagan

Via: Director of Central Intelligence (DCI), William J. Casey

Subject: Results of investigation into Operation Urgent Fury paranormal incident

1. On 25 October 1983 the invasion of Grenada began under the designation Operation Urgent Fury.

2. The operation was approved by POTUS to: 1) Rescue U.S. citizens on the island, 2) dislodge communist combat forces, 3) reinstate pro U.S. leadership. The last two goals

were authorized by the Top Secret classified National Security Decision Directive (NSDD) 110A.[1]

3. By 26 October 1983 all three objectives were achieved and the operation was declared completed by the joint task force commander, Vice Admiral Joseph Metcalf, U.S. Navy.

4. During the operation, units from the Army Special Operations component of the joint task force were diverted to conduct reconnaissance of sites suspected to be associated with the hostage-taking of British nationals.[2]

5. The force made contact with an unknown and unassociated hostile force and took heavy casualties, including some killed-in-action, and resulted in the complete destruction of a corporate research facility.

6. Following standard protocol, the survivors were debriefed immediately and have been notified of potential criminal charges for violating non-disclosure agreements.

---

[1] National security directives are generally classified and directed only to the National Security Council and the most senior executive branch officials, and focus on foreign and military policy-making guidance.

[2] The Army Special Operations Command (USASOC) would not be created until 1988, at which point units such as the Rangers, Special Forces "Green Berets," Task Force 160, Civil Affairs, and PSYOPs would be organized under a more formal command and control structure.

7. POTUS designated CIA-OIG the lead investigatory body and ordered a full report and briefing within a year of the incident.

8. The information contained in this report represents a complete and chronological breakdown of the events as they unfolded, including intelligence collected on the ground and subsequent documentation aggregated from multiple associated organizations.[3]

---

[3] This is a certified copy of the original file. All documentation has been accounted for and no information has been redacted.

FACT SHEET: 75TH INFANTRY REGIMENT (RANGER)

○　　　　　　○

United States Army
Instructional Product

The 75th Infantry Regiment (Ranger) is an elite force designed to rapidly deploy anywhere in the world within 18 hours to conduct scalable commando-style missions by land, sea, or air. The Rangers are the oldest special operations unit in the United States, as the term is defined today. Ranger units began operating in North America in the colonial period prior to the founding of the country, and have been involved in every U.S. conflict since.

The modern Ranger force was first established during World War II with the famed Ranger Battalions. The 1st, 2nd, 3rd, 4th, and 5th Ranger Battalions served in the Atlantic theater, serving as the spearhead for the North African and Italian campaigns in addition to the Normandy invasion. The 6th Ranger Battalion, and the 5307th Composite Unit (Provisional) known as "Merrill's Marauders," served in the Pacific theater conducting deep penetration raids and prisoner of war rescue missions.

After World War II, the Army disbanded the battalions in favor of a return to stand-alone Ranger companies designed to support conventional operations. The Korean War saw the formation of 16 of these companies which all saw intense combat and served a variety of functions from scouting and ambushing missions to raids that destroyed major enemy headquarters. This conflict would mark the first time that Rangers attended airborne training and utilized the skillset to insert behind enemy lines.

After the Vietnam War, individual Long Range Reconnaissance Patrol (LRRP) companies attached to conventional divisions were combined to form the 1st and 2nd Battalions of the 75th Infantry Regiment. To distinguish the regiment from others, it was given the "(Ranger)" designation. Prior to the invasion of Grenada, plans were underway to expand the regiment to include a 3rd Battalion and to officially name the unit the 75th Ranger Regiment.[4]

Each Ranger Battalion is made up of four companies of approximately 150 Rangers each. They are trained to conduct: parachute assaults, mountain warfare, small boat operations, long range reconnaissance, and other mission sets that require the Rangers' unique blend of speed, surprise, and violence of action.

---

[4] While many members of the Ranger Regiment are graduates of the infamous Ranger School, readers should note that these are wholly separate organizations that share a common name but serve very different purposes.

Members of the Ranger Regiment are assessed and selected to serve as combat forces in a special operations unit. They are identified by a red and black Ranger "scroll" patch.

Students of Ranger School can be from any unit, conventional or special operations. They are trained in small unit tactics and graded in various positions of leadership. Graduates are identified by a black and yellow Ranger "tab" patch.

KEY WITNESS DOSSIERS

○   ○

Central Intelligence Agency
Office of the Inspector General (OIG)
Langley, VA

October 1984

(By order of appearance)

	**Name**	Mr. Christopher Seward
	Age	52
	Home of Record	St. George's, Grenada
	Citizenship	United Kingdom

Employer and Position

Essex Agricultural & Petrochemical Limited; Assistant Vice
President of Research

Professional *Curriculum Vitae*

- 1953, Graduated University of St Andrews
- 1953, Employed by British Petroleum
- 1965, Employed by Essex A&P Ltd.

Background Notes

Seward was an accomplished chemist at a young age. His undergraduate work at St. Andrews earned him the attention of several major corporations who seemed to have steered his motivations away from scientific discovery and towards business management. After early success, his career has since stalled. He has been posted to Grenada for over ten years, and it can be assumed that he is apathetic about his job. He has been divorced three times; court filings show they were all quite bitter. He is presumed to be estranged from his adult daughter.

Following the incident in Grenada, Seward continues his employment with Essex A&P.

*****

Name	Geoff Holme
Age	19
Home of Record	West Covina, CA
Rank	Private First Class
Position	Combat Medic (68W)

Organization:

Headquarters, F Company, 1st Battalion, 75th Infantry Regiment (Ranger), U.S. Army

Service History:

- 1982, Graduated Basic Training
- 1982, Graduated Airborne School
- 1982, Assigned to 1st Battalion, 75th Infantry Regiment (Ranger)

Awards:

Purple Heart Medal, Armed Forces Expeditionary Medal w/ arrowhead device, Parachutist Badge w/ combat jump device, Combat Medical Badge (Nothing else follows).

Background Notes:

An only child, Holme's father passed away in a car accident when he was just six. His mother is a public school librarian and moonlights as a night-shift hotel manager. He had a number of minor interactions with law enforcement as a juvenile. His most serious offense was a vandalism charge that resulted in community service at a local free clinic. This may have inspired him to become a medic, as he had no further legal issues and soon thereafter enlisted in the Rangers.

Following the incident in Grenada, Holme separated from the Army in March 1984.

*****

Name	Derrick McClelland
Age	34
Home of Record	North Canton, OH
Rank	Sergeant First Class
Position	Infantry Platoon Sergeant (11B)

Organization:

3rd Platoon, F Company, 1st Battalion, 75th Infantry Regiment (Ranger), U.S. Army

Service History:

- 1968, Drafted
- 1968, Graduated Basic Training
- 1968, Assigned to 1st Infantry Division
- 1969, Assigned to I Co./75th Infantry Regiment (LRRP)
- 1972, Graduated Ranger School
- 1973, Graduated Airborne School
- 1974, Assigned to 1st Battalion, 75th Infantry Regiment (Ranger)

Awards:

Silver Star Medal, Purple Heart Medal x3, Bronze Star Medal w/ valor device, Army Commendation Medal x2, Army Achievement Medal x2, Armed Forces Expeditionary Medal w/ arrowhead device, Vietnam Campaign Medal, Vietnam Service Medal, Parachutist Badge w/ combat jump device, Combat Infantryman's Badge, Ranger Tab (Nothing else follows).

Background Notes:

While serving in Vietnam, McClelland distinguished himself numerous times and volunteered for the LRRP teams. Afterward, he helped form the newly reconstituted Ranger Battalions. He and his wife married in Hawaii during R&R in 1969, and they have three teenage children.[5] He is up for

---

[5] "R&R" is an abbreviation for Rest & Relaxation, a mid-tour break that is given to servicemembers halfway through their year-long combat deployment.

retirement in 1988. Prior to the Grenada invasion, his Battalion Commander commented on his last NCO evaluation report, "SFC McClelland is a living legend who has mentored the next generation of Rangers and for that I'm confident they are ready for any mission our country may ask of them."[6]

Following the incident in Grenada, McClelland took a position in the Ranger Training Brigade to close out his career.

*****

Name	Theodore Shepherd
Age	25
Home of Record	Falls Church, VA
Rank	First Lieutenant
Position	Infantry Platoon Leader (11A)

Organization:

3rd Platoon, F Company, 1st Battalion, 75th Infantry Regiment (Ranger), U.S. Army

---

[6] Non-commissioned Officers, or "NCOs," are enlisted leaders in the Army with the rank of Corporal through Sergeant Major. Not to be confused with commissioned officers, who are traditionally college graduates holding the ranks of Second Lieutenant through General.

Service History:

- 1979, Graduated U.S. Military Academy at West Point
- 1979, Graduated Infantry Officer Basic Course
- 1979, Graduated Airborne School
- 1980, Assigned to 2nd Brigade, 82nd Airborne Division[7]
- 1981, Graduated Ranger School
- 1982, Assigned to 1st Battalion, 75th Infantry Regiment (Ranger)

Awards:

Bronze Star w/ valor device, Army Commendation Medal, Army Achievement Medal, Armed Forces Expeditionary Medal w/ arrowhead device, Parachutist Badge w/ combat jump device, Combat Infantryman's Badge, Ranger Tab (Nothing else follows).

Background Notes:

Shepherd's father was a General officer and retired from the Pentagon. He was an Eagle Scout and played varsity baseball. While lifeguarding one summer in high school, he saved the life of a senator's granddaughter and it made the local D.C. news. He was subsequently invited to the White House and met President Nixon. His classmates at West Point identified him as

---

[7] Prior to taking command in the Rangers, officers must complete a successful tour of duty in an equivalent position in the conventional Army. In this case, Shepherd served as a platoon leader in the 82nd Airborne Division prior to joining the elite Rangers.

"competent, yet uniquely ambitious." He was runner up for the Distinguished Honor Graduate award in Ranger School.[8] He is newly married to a Duke University grad he met while stationed at Fort Bragg. Her father is a district court judge with deep familial ties to the coastal Carolina region.

Following the incident in Grenada, Shepherd became a company commander in the 82nd Airborne Division.

---

[8] The William O. Darby Distinguished Honor Graduate award is named after the founder of the 1st Ranger Battalion who stood up the force in 1942 and led them in the invasion of North Africa during World War II.

WEATHER BULLETIN

National Weather Service
National Hurricane Center
Miami, FL

September 11, 1983

000
ABNT20 KNHC 081709
TWOAT

Tropical Weather Outlook
NWS National Hurricane Center Miami FL
200 PM EDT Sat Sep 11 1983

For the North Atlantic...Caribbean Sea and the Gulf of
Mexico:

**Tropical Depression Six formation is expected to cause
heavy rainfall in the Lesser Antilles,** before degenerating
into an open tropical wave on September 20 near the
Dominican Republic.

$$

Forecaster Nelson

○   ○

"Cultivate crop yields, not crop outbreaks."

Essex A&P Ltd. | London | January 1982

Controlling the risks to equatorial farming.

In the age of increased globalization and commerce, crops are exposed to more threats than ever before. Along with transporting valuable imports and exports serving as the lifeblood of Caribbean nations, massive container ships can also bring new adversaries to agriculture.

The equatorial climate is uniquely conducive to incubating strains of fungal and bacterial threats. These are the silent menace to crop yields and can start deep inside the plant before manifesting as wilting, browning, molding, and rotting. The tropics are also home to an infinite number of parasitic insects and competitive plant species that prey on fields by stealing resources and choking life from viable plants.

A legacy of success, a culture of innovation.

At Essex A&P, we work tirelessly to create tailored products that aid farmers, but are also safe for the food supply and our environment. Founded in 1899 by two brothers in a humble garden shed, Essex A&P is now a global powerhouse of scientific research and development with offices in 32 countries.

Essex A&P pioneers modern processes which allow synthesizing of cutting edge products honed through historical trial and error. These breakthroughs are often made possible by identifying regionally effective treatments and preventative solutions based on indigenous knowledge.

Pufferfish are representative of the local species used in our innovation.

Pairing Ancient Compounds with Modern Science.

From the island of Hispaniola comes a chemical compound more commonly associated with Voodoo rituals than with crop preservation. In their folklore, a combination of the neurotoxin found in pufferfish (Tetrodotoxin) and samples of a poison from plants of the nightshade family (Datura) could be used to reanimate a person and place them under the control of another as a servant. Despite their historical association with colorful activities of the occult, these compounds provide an efficient foundation for increasing crop performance.

Jimsonweed or the "Devil's Trumpet" is known to contain Datura.

The First All-in-one that's One-for-all.

The Zumbithren© all-in-one plant defender is specially formulated to protect tropical horticulture. The tetrodotoxin element stops plant-killing insects and pathogens, while datura naturally wards away any plant competition. Standard harvesting and consumption preparation processes ensure that there are no side effects for humans or the environment.

The proprietary blend is also effective for all crops. No reformulation is necessary, simplifying purchasing and storage considerations.

Zumbithren© is already tested and approved by your country's health service for the following:

Bananas	Coffee	Rubber tree
Barley	Maize	Sugarcane
Cacao	Palms	Sweet potato
Chickpea	Papaya	Taro
Coconut	Rice	Yam

Want to learn more? Contact us to be referred to your local Essex A&P sales executive. Toll Free Number: 1-800-867-5309

SITUATION REPORT

O   O

Central Intelligence Agency
Office of Latin American Analysis
Langley, VA

October 1983

Background

Grenada was made an official colony of the British Empire in 1877, having previously been colonized by both the French and the British as early as 1649. Independence was granted in 1974 and came under the leadership of the first Prime Minister of Grenada. Grenada opted to remain within the Commonwealth of Nations, represented locally by a governor-general (a largely ceremonial position) and retained the Queen of England as their monarch. This arraignment is similar to those of many other Caribbean nations.

Political Upheaval

Conflict broke out between the government and opposition parties. During the 1976 Grenadian general election, the opposition claimed that fraud and intimidation was performed by the militia loyal to the Prime Minister and deemed the results invalid.

In March 1979, while the Prime Minister was out of the country, his opposition launched a coup which removed him and suspended the constitution. Maurice Bishop, who declared himself Prime Minister, then established the People's Revolutionary Government. To give the appearance of legitimacy, the new administration continued to recognize Governor-General Paul Scoon as the representative of the Commonwealth and the Queen of England. Bishop's Marxist–Leninist government established close ties with Cuba, Nicaragua, and other communist bloc countries. All other political parties were banned and no elections were held during the four years of Bishop's rule.

Escalating Violence

On October 16, 1983, Bishop's Deputy Prime Minister seized power and placed him under house arrest. Mass protests against this coup led to Bishop escaping detention and reasserting his authority as the head of the government. Bishop was recaptured and murdered by a firing squad of soldiers, along with his wife and several government officials and union leaders loyal to him. The army then stepped in and formed a military council to rule the country, placing Governor-General Scoon under house arrest. The army announced a four-day total curfew during which anyone seen on the streets would be summarily executed.

U.S. Interests

First, the Organization of Eastern Caribbean States (OECS) have all directly appealed to the United States for assistance in restoring order to Grenada. Although under captivity, Governor-General Scoon has also requested U.S. intervention through diplomatic channels, using the reserve powers vested in his position to encourage an invasion and his rescue.

Additionally, POTUS has voiced concerns over "the 600 U.S. medical students on the island" and worries of a repeat of the Iran hostage crisis.

Finally, the pro-Communist government under Bishop has constructed facilities to aid a Soviet-Cuban military buildup in the Caribbean. The jewel among those projects is a 9,000-foot runway with the capacity to accommodate the Soviet's largest aircraft. Such a facility could enhance the Soviet and Cuban transportation of weapons to Central American insurgents and expand Soviet regional influence in the western hemisphere.

FIGURE 1. GEOGRAPHIC MAP OF GRENADA

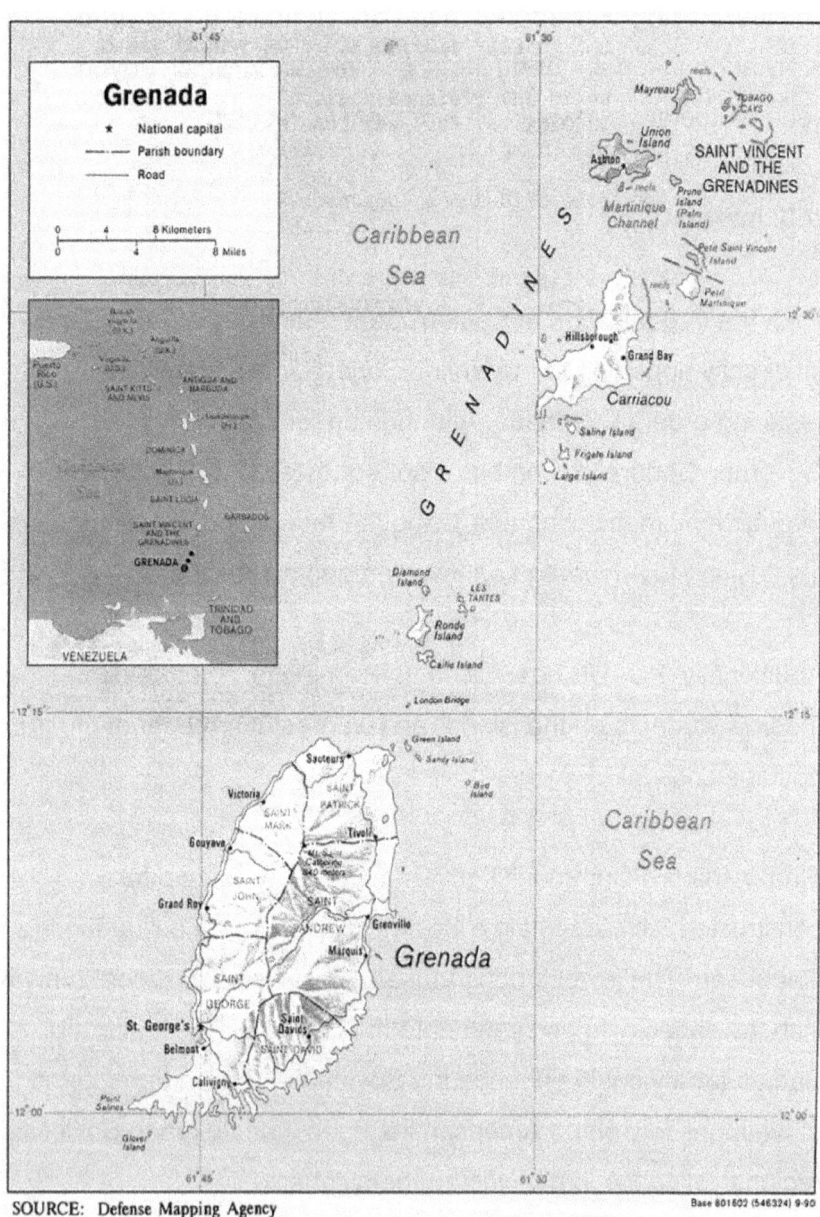

SOURCE: Defense Mapping Agency

Base 801602 (546324) 9-90

COUNTRY REPORT

Central Intelligence Agency
Office of Latin American Analysis
Langley, VA

October 1983

Grenada is an island between the Caribbean Sea and Atlantic Ocean, north of Trinidad and Tobago. Comparatively, it is twice the size of Washington, D.C.

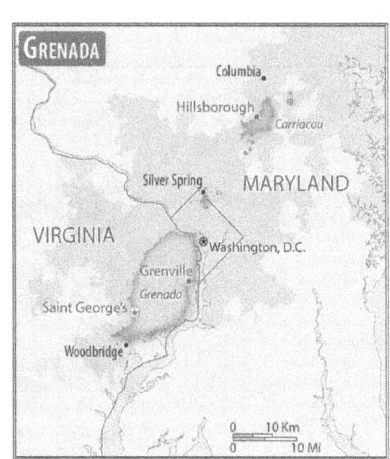

Population Distribution: approximately one-third of the population is found in the capital of St. George's; the island's population is concentrated along the coast.

Population	114,299
Ethnic Groups	African descent 82.4%, Mixed 13.3%, East Indian 2.2%, Other 1.3%, Unspecified 0.9%
Language	English (official), French patois
Coastline	121 km
Climate	Tropical; tempered by northeast trade winds
Terrain	Volcanic in origin with central mountains
Natural Resources	Timber, tropical fruit
Natural Hazards	Lies on edge of hurricane belt; hurricane season lasts from June to November

The flag of the nation of Grenada.

MAINTENANCE REPORT

O   O

Essex A&P Ltd.
Ronde Island Facility
Grenada

Maintenance Log

Date of Report:	October 15, 1983
Reporter:	David Pottinger, Facilities Manager
Found During:	[ ] Scheduled Maintenance [X] Callout Request
Issue Status:	[X] Corrected Immediately [ ] Parts on order [ ] Full replacement required

Issue Description:

Got a call from the dormitory closest to the water treatment

plant that their tap water tastes funny. Truth be told, I'd

noticed a change in the water quality myself over the past few weeks. Checked the plant and everything appeared to be running fine. I had two guys change out all the filters ahead of schedule just to be safe. There was no change to the water quality.

I had the guys inspect the water lines and they discovered a cross contamination issue by the #36 storm drain over by the chemical storage area. Apparently, there was a leaking container that was isolated to its paddock. I'm guessing that the heavy rains in September created a stream of water that carried the pool of chemicals into our drainage system that is reclaimed for potable use.

The container isn't labeled in plain english, so I wrote down what was inside (Datura and Tetrodotoxin) and sent a memo to the head of the Research Division, Paul Hamm, and to the facility's medic for their awareness.

We placed the leaking container into a larger one that is sealed for now. We'll plan to build a berm around the Chemical Storage area to avoid a similar issue in the future.[9] Has only been a day since we made the fix and the drinking water is already back to normal. - David P.

---

[9] A berm is a high, unsupported earthen wall.

TELEPHONE INTERCEPT ONE

National Security Agency
National SIGINT Operations Center
Fort Meade, MD

Intercepted Telephone Recording

Date Recorded - October 17, 1983

Names mentioned:
- Christopher Seward - Associate Vice President, Research
- David Pottinger - Facilities Manager
- Dr. Paul Hamm - Head Researcher

Locations:
- Originating: Rhonde Island, Grenada
- Receiving: London, U.K.

```
1                    :Telephone Line Ringing:


2        [Hamm]      This is Paul Hamm. Christopher, is
```

that you?

3   [Seward]   Yes, Paul. Hello. What is so
                        pressing that it can't wait until
                        I'm back in Grenada?

4   [Hamm]   Christopher, I've got David
                        Pottinger from Facilities here on
                        speaker. We need to discuss a
                        serious issue his team found.

5   [Pottinger]   Yeah, hi Chris. How're things back
                        in London?

6   [Seward]   …it's Christopher. Things are
                        splendid. I canceled dinner
                        reservations at The Ivy to talk to
                        you fine gentlemen tonight.

                        What can I do for you, David?

7   [Pottinger]   Uh, yes. Sorry, Christopher. Uh…

8   [Hamm]   To get to the point, the
                        facility's potable water has been
                        contaminated. The recent storms
                        down here washed out sections of
                        our chemical storage bays and
                        leached the raw compounds for our

newest agricultural product into the system.

9   [Seward]   Wouldn't the water plant filter out any contaminants?

10 [Hamm]   That's the real issue. These compounds can bypass any filtration we do.

11 [Seward]   How could this happen! David, do we not pay your men to conduct infrastructure inspections!

12 [Pottinger]   Uh, yes Christopher. But our backlogs have only grown since you insisted on major renovations to the main villa, and...

13 [Seward]   Ohhhh, I see. This is somehow MY fault and not the fault of the MAINTENANCE workers who get paid to MAINTAIN!

14 [Pottinger]   Chris, I mean Christopher. That's not how I meant it!

15 [Hamm]   Christopher, nevermind that! We have bigger problems here. People are going to get very sick. We

need to call in the Grenadian
health department and begin to
evacuate these people off the
island.

16   [Seward]   Absolutely not! We will manage
this in-house. What is the point
of employing all these doctors and
scientists if we can't treat a
simple case of tainted water?

17   [Hamm]   This is much more serious than
just putting out a boil water
advisory. I think there could be
potentially deadly ramifications
of such prolonged exposure to the
compounds.

18   [Seward]   How long was the exposure?!

19   [Pottinger]   The storms came through in
mid-September. The leaching was
going on for at least a couple
weeks. We were busy cleaning up
other issues, and…

20   [Seward]   David, if I could reach through
this bloody phone and strangle
you, I would. Do you realize that

I have to present an update in front of the Board of Directors in the morning? I will not lose this job because you dimwits couldn't manage some rainwater!

21   [Hamm]   I think this is a big mistake, Christopher.

22   [Seward]   Well I think this is a massive liability issue, *Paul.* I think everyone who is sick is going to ask how they got sick, *Paul.* I think an incident like this will scare the Board and make them rethink the type of research you are doing, *Paul.*

Do you understand what I'm getting at?

23   [Hamm]   What would you have us do?

24   [Seward]   Blame it on our produce vendor from the mainland. Tell everyone it is just a serious case of food poisoning. Fire the vendor immediately.

Is the contamination cleaned up already?

25 [Pottinger] Yes, Christopher. It's not a problem anymore.

26 [Seward] Well, that is the first good news I've heard.

If we don't make a big deal about this then it won't become one. Treat the sick as needed and they will get over it.

27 [Hamm] I really believe that we may lose some people from this.

28 [Seward] Well I guess you better get off the phone and go assist in the infirmary then. I am now late for my second set of dinner reservations for the evening.

I trust you can handle it from here. I'll be back in Grenada next week.

29 :Telephone Line Disconnected:

SECTION TWO: FIRST-CONTACT

The following section details the initial combat action experienced by the highlighted unit and tracks how the unit was subsequently retasked to intervene in the paranormal incident.

INVASION OPERATIONS ORDER

O   O

Department of the Army
1st Battalion, 75th Infantry Regiment (Ranger)
Hunter Army Airfield, GA

20 OCTOBER 1983

Situation

The nation of Grenada has been occupied by local
revolutionaries and Cuban communist forces, deposing a
government friendly to U.S. interests and trapping more
than 600 U.S. citizens attending St. George's University in
a volatile security situation. The students are at high risk of
becoming political hostages. Additionally, long-range
Soviet bombing and transport assets could utilize the
country's large airports to threaten the U.S. if allowed to
remain long term.

Enemy Disposition

- Grenadian People's Revolutionary Army (PRA) - 1,500 Grenadian soldiers are manning defensive positions. The PRA troops are equipped with light weapons, mostly AK-47 rifles and smaller numbers of carbines and submachine guns. They have few heavy weapons and no modern air defense systems. The PRA possesses eight armored personnel carriers, two armored cars, and no tanks.
- Cuba - We assess there to be an estimated 800 combat troops on Grenada disguised as construction workers.
- Advisor and observer support - We assess there to be an estimated 100 liaisons total from the Soviet Union, North Korea, East Germany, and Libya on the island enabling the PRA.

Enemy Locations and Missions of Adjacent Units

- Point Salines International Airport - Primary foothold and airbridge for invasion. To be secured by Army Ranger elements.

- Pearls Airport - Secondary foothold and airbridge for invasion. To be secured by Marine Corps elements.

- True Blue & Grand Anse Campuses of St. George's University - Location of an estimated 600 American medical students held hostage. To be secured by Army Ranger elements.

- Richmond Hill Prison - Political prisoner hostage site. To be secured by Army Special Missions Unit (SMU) and Ranger elements.[10]

- Governor-General Mansion - Where Paul Scoon, family, and staff are believed to be held under house arrest. To be secured by Navy SEAL elements.

- Fort Rupert - Headquarters for enemy leadership. To be secured by Army SMU and Ranger elements.

- Fort Frederick - Major coordination site and armory for enemy forces. To be secured by Marine Corps elements.

- Radio Free Grenada Station - Key enemy mass communication channel. To be secured by Navy SEAL elements.

---

[10] A Special Missions Unit is a highly classified, selective, and well-resourced force that specializes in clandestine activities of national importance.

Mission

1st Battalion will seize the Point Salines International Airport in order to establish a foothold for the invasion and enable follow-on forces to conduct forcible entry operations and facilitate the extraction of U.S. citizens in the vicinity of the True Blue Medical Campus. After completing the noncombatant evacuation operation (NEO), units will standby for follow on taskings.

Execution

Commander's Intent

1st Battalion will assault the Point Salines airfield on the southern end of the island and destroy all enemy forces occupying the area. After establishing a perimeter, they will move to rescue all U.S. citizens at the medical school. Endstate: Airfield is secured with minimal destruction to infrastructure, U.S. citizens are safely evacuated from the nearby university campus, and all enemy forces in the area are destroyed.

Concept of the Operation

- A and B Companies will clear and hold the main terminal and outlying administrative buildings and hangars.
- C and D Companies will isolate the airfield and create a perimeter.
- E and F Companies will clear the airfield of any obstructions, serve as reinforcements for A-D Companies' objectives, and prepare to execute the NEO of the True Blue Campus.

Fire support available from orbiting AC-130s and naval gunfire on standby from the destroyer USS *Caron*.

Service and Support

The support company will coordinate the distribution of material for three days of sustainment, to include:

- Parachutes
- Ammunition
- Rations
- Water

The battalion aid station will coordinate the distribution of:

- Medic aid bags and individual bleed out kits
- Drugs and I.V. equipment

- Motion sickness pills

Command and Control

The Operation Urgent Fury commander is Admiral Metcalf of the 2nd Fleet. He will be located on the aircraft carrier USS Independence (CV-6) during the invasion. The 75th Infantry Regiment (Ranger) headquarters element will be located at the Point Salines International Airport main terminal after it is secured.

FIGURE 2. INVASION PLANNING MAP OF GRENADA

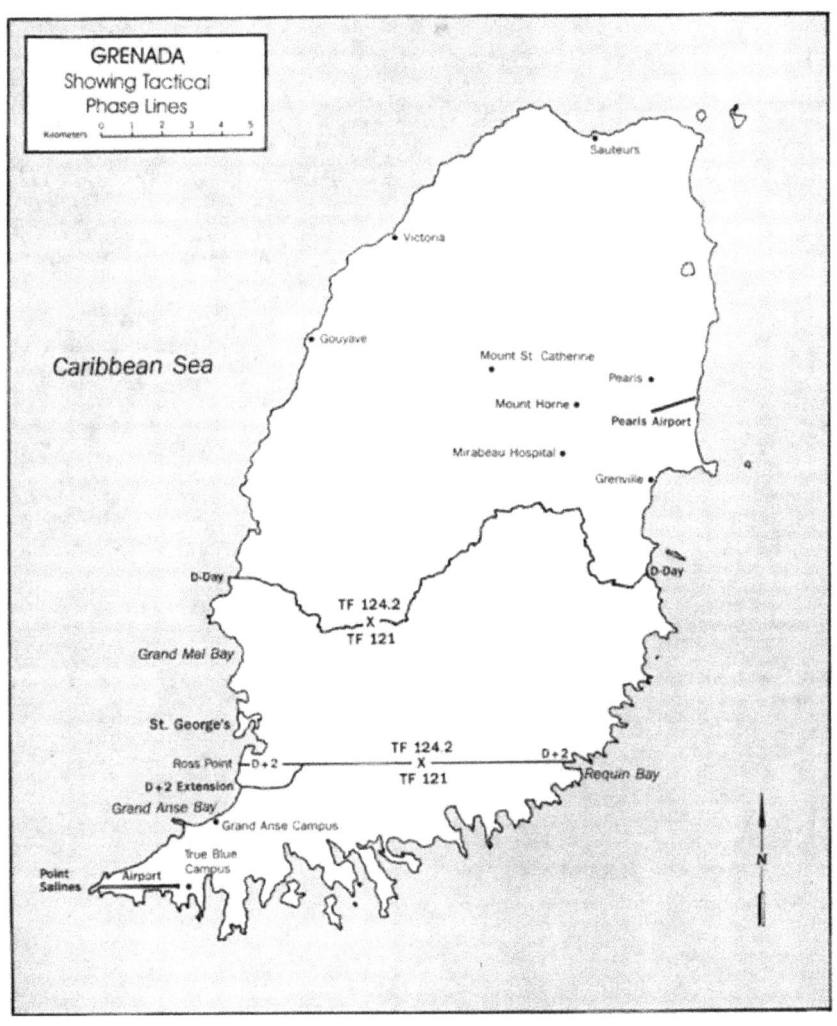

FIGURE 3. AERIAL IMAGERY OF POINT SALINES AIRPORT

POL Storage Area

Hardy Bay

New Cuban
Housing Area

Medical School

140

64

FACT SHEET: AIRFIELD SEIZURE

United States Army
Instructional Product

Joint forcible entry (JFE) operations seize and hold footholds against an armed opposition. A foothold, or lodgement, is a designated area in a hostile or potentially hostile operational area (such as an airhead) that affords continuous landing of troops and materiel while providing maneuver space for subsequent operations. There are two critical decisions during the first phase of an airfield seizure, to airdrop or airland. The commander bases this decision upon obstacles and threats to aircraft in the vicinity of the objective area.

Point Salines International Airport as seen from the air.

In the airland option, the transport aircraft land on the objective airfield and the troops deploy from the aircraft once on the ground. The advantage of the airland insertion is that drop-related casualties are avoided and units can deploy in a more organized fashion. The disadvantage is that this method is highly dependent upon a secured objective and unobstructed runways and taxiways.

In the airdrop scenario, an overwhelming airborne force conducts a mass tactical parachute assault directly onto the contested facility to occupy by force.[11] Once secured, follow-on forces use

---

[11] In a mass tactical airborne insertion, the aircraft approach the drop zone low and in close formation to ensure the force is deployed as quickly and close together as possible in order to minimize the vulnerable time over the contested area.

the airfield to establish the airbridge that facilitates the deployment of additional forces and logistics. The success of these missions is heavily reliant on air superiority and suppression of enemy air defenses (SEAD).

In both options, once on the airfield the forces clear any obstructions or threats and secure the objective, pushing out to create a perimeter to defend against counterattack.

Rangers seizing Point Salines International Airport on 25 October 1983.

INTERVIEW TRANSCRIPT ONE

Department of the Army
Office of the Deputy Chief of Staff for Intelligence G-2
Washington, DC

Interview Recording Transcript - Session 1
Interview Date: 31 OCT 1983
Interviewer: Major Simon Conner, Counterintelligence Section
Interviewee: PFC Geoff Holme, 1/75th Rangers

	:Transcript Begins:
MAJ Conner	(Static)...do you understand these rights as I've read them to you?
PFC Holme	Yes, sir. I do.
MAJ Conner	Let the record reflect that Private First Class Holme has been advised of his rights and he acknowledges them.

	Let's start with the alert. When were you first informed of the upcoming invasion?
PFC Holme	Two nights prior to the jump, I was asleep in my barracks room when there was a pounding on my door. The company CQ runner was going down the halls yelling that we were going to war.[12] We started preparing and the platoon got regular updates before we went south.
MAJ Conner	At that time, were you made aware of the unconventional mission your platoon would eventually be tasked with?
PFC Holme	No, sir.
MAJ Conner	Was it brought up at all in those early days that you might be looking for the staff from Essex A&P?

---

[12] "CQ" stands for Charge of Quarters. This is a small, rotating duty section that guards the company area at all times. The "runner" is the most junior member of the team whose job is to pass messages in person when necessary.

| PFC Holme | Maybe the leadership knew that, but I don't think that info made its way to me.

To be honest, I was still pretty new and had enough on my mind at the time just prepping for the jump. Actually, I was freaked out. Only a year prior, I was in high school and now I was going to invade Grenada with the Rangers. |
|---|---|
| MAJ Conner | Okay. Tell me about that parachute assault. |
| PFC Holme | The original plan was to just land at the airport and secure it that way. On the flight over from Georgia, we got word that the Cubans had blocked the runway with heavy construction equipment and we'd have to jump in. |
| MAJ Conner | That had to be pretty intense. Do you think that might have been tough, psychologically speaking, on you and the other Rangers in your platoon? |
| PFC Holme | Personally, I was too busy worrying about messing up. It was extremely hectic in the aircraft as equipment was being passed out |

	and everyone was rigging up in their parachute harnesses.[13] The inside of the C-130 isn't that large, and it was a tight squeeze. I *was* scared though. I won't lie and say I wasn't.
MAJ Conner	Perfectly understandable, Holme.
PFC Holme	So the aircraft comes in low from the ocean and the ride gets really bumpy. I'm a jumper on the left side of the aircraft, so when the doors open I have a good view of the island to the north of us. I could actually see tracer fire from anti-aircraft artillery.
MAJ Conner	(Whistles) Just like the Normandy invasion, huh?
PFC Holme	I'll admit, for a split second the thought did cross my mind. It was surreal.

---

[13] "Rigging up" is the methodical process of donning a parachute harness and attaching one's combat equipment to it. A buddy system is used to rig up initially, followed by a comprehensive quality check performed by experts called Jumpmasters. Only after this check is a jumper prepared to exit the aircraft.

	Anyway, we're right over the runway, and I see the light go green.[14] The guys in front of me start moving forward. The next thing I know, I'm at the door handing off my static line.[15] I'm up-and-out, it's loud with rushing wind, and I'm counting.[16] I feel the tug of the parachute opening, and I have just enough time to check that my canopy looks good when I look down to see the ground. Then, I smashed into a taxiway.
MAJ Conner	Does that hurt?
PFC Holme	Hell yes, sir! It hurts...a lot.

---

[14] Jumpers can see a set of lights similar to a traffic signal in the aircraft that serves as a visual indicator of when to exit.

[15] The static line is a cord that connects the parachute to the aircraft. As the jumper exits and falls to the earth, the cord pulls the parachute open automatically. This is different from freefall parachuting whereby jumpers are responsible for opening their parachutes manually at a prescribed altitude.

[16] Paratroopers are taught to count aloud after they exit the aircraft. If they reach a certain number and they still feel as though their parachute is not open, they need to open their reserve parachute to save themselves.

	After my body stops vibrating from the impact, I get up and join the Rangers around me to clear the obstacles from the runway.
MAJ Conner	So your platoon didn't do much shooting at the airport?
PFC Holme	No, sir. A few of our folks returned fire after landing initially. As the drop zone got crowded and the other companies organized to clear the buildings, we focused on our part of the mission. There was plenty of fighting going on to secure the airport but me and my guys were focused on getting that runway open again for follow-on forces. The other units ended up surrounding a large enemy force in one of the hangers and getting them to surrender anyway.
MAJ Conner	Yes, I'd heard about that. Okay. Let's take a break. (Chairs screeching)
PFC Holme	Yes, sir.
	:Transcript Ends:

WITNESS STATEMENT ONE

SWORN STATEMENT
For use of this form, see AR 190-45.

LOCATION	DATE (YYYMMDD)	TIME	FILE NUMBER
USA	19831031	0900	

LAST NAME, FIRST NAME, MIDDLE NAME	GRADE/STATUS
McClelland, Derrick, NMN	E-7 / RA

ORGANIZATION OR ADDRESS

3rd PLT, F Co., 1/75 INF REG (Ranger), Hunter Army Airfield, GA

I, SFC Derrick McClelland , WANT TO MAKE THE FOLLOWING STATEMENT UNDER OATH:

During the invasion of Grenada, I was a platoon sergeant

assisting with the evacuation of American citizens from the

"True Blue" campus when I became aware of a potential outbreak at the Essex A&P research facility.

After securing the airport, my platoon moved to the St. George's University Medical College just to the east of our location. We encountered some resistance (some Rangers in another company were killed) but ultimately made our way onto the campus which was lightly defended. We immediately began to clear through the different administrative offices, lecture halls, and dormitories. We found students had barricaded themselves to hide from the enemy forces. They were extremely happy to see us and compliant as we guided them to safety.

The hostages were all in good spirits and unharmed with the exception of one man who was brought to my attention. The man had been shot in the abdomen and was being treated at the medical college. The man identified himself as David Pottinger, and he informed us that he was not a student or staff member of the university.

What he said next alarmed me, "They're killing each other on Rhonde Island." I took that to mean that the PRA and the Cubans had turned on each other, so I asked him if he saw them shooting at each other. He said, "No, not the soldiers. The people are eating each other." His wounds were severe, he was very weak, and he spoke with great difficulty. I was very confused by his statement so I asked him to explain.

He said that he was a maintenance worker at a company called Essex A&P at their research facility on Rhonde Island. As he told it, there had been some kind of chemical spill that was infecting all the workers. The sickness made them violent and attack one another. He decided to make a run for the docks to escape by boat which was apparently against the orders of his management. The managers there wanted to keep what was happening a secret. As he sailed off, someone fired at him and struck him in the abdomen.

Once he got back to the mainland, he went to tell the police but the coup was causing chaos. He decided to make his way down to the medical school for treatment. He heard rumors that a group of Essex A&P survivors were captured by the PRA near Fort Frederick.

His story was unbelievable, but I passed it along to my platoon leader, 1LT Shepherd. David was evacuated on a flight to the U.S., but I was later informed that he died enroute.

AFFIDAVIT

I HAVE READ OR HAVE HAD READ TO ME THIS STATEMENT. I FULLY UNDERSTAND THE CONTENTS OF THE ENTIRE STATEMENT MADE BY ME. THE STATEMENT IS TRUE. I HAVE MADE THIS STATEMENT FREELY WITHOUT HOPE OF BENEFIT OR REWARD, WITHOUT THREAT OF PUNISHMENT, AND WITHOUT COERCION, UNLAWFUL INFLUENCE, OR UNLAWFUL INDUCEMENT.

Derrick McClelland 31 OCT 83

(Signature of Person Making Statement)

INITIALS OF PERSON MAKING STATEMENT

DM

PAGE

2 OF 2

DA FORM 2814, DEC 1979

FRAGMENTARY ORDER ONE

Department of the Army
1st Battalion, 75th Infantry Regiment (Ranger)
Hunter Army Airfield, GA

25 OCTOBER 1983

Situation

S-2 received reports that there may be a group of British
nationals from the Essex A&P company being held
hostage at a hospital near Fort Frederick.[17] Units from the
task force are already engaged with securing that area so
additional assets must be pulled from the southern area of
responsibility to support the evacuation of these

---

[17] "S-2" stands for the intelligence staff. Military staff elements are
organized numerically, prefixed with an "S" for staff, according to
historical tradition that dates back to the 19th century. 1 = Personnel, 2 =
Intelligence, 3 = Operations, 4 = Logistics, 5 = Plans, 6 = Signals, and on.

individuals. Reportedly many of them are sick or injured and will require ambulatory assistance.

Enemy Disposition
- Enemy strength at the hospital is believed to be light, equipped with small arms only
- Expect roving patrols and sentries both inside and outside the building
- Nearby Fort Frederick has a large enemy garrison armed with heavy weapons and light armored vehicles that can quickly respond to the hospital

Mission

O/o F Co., 1/75 detaches a platoon to isolate IVO Fort Frederick garrison to facilitate clearance and safeguard any British nationals held there.

Execution

Commander's Intent

A team from the SMU will be the main effort in clearing the objective and securing the British nationals. A platoon from F company will support by isolating the objective area, repelling any potential counterattack, and providing litter carriers for any non-ambulatory evacuees. Endstate: All hostages are found and returned to the airport.

Concept of the Operation

- Link up with the team from the SMU and aircrew from Task Force 160 at Point Salines airport
- Move to the objective area via four (4) MH-60 Blackhawks and land immediately adjacent to the target building
- Isolate the target building in preparation for the main effort assault and prevent ingress/egress of enemy forces or potential hostages
- Post-assault, provide litter carrier assistance enroute to the Pickup Zone (PZ)
- Transfer hostages to advanced medical care upon return to the Point Salines airport

Fire support will be available from x1 MH-60 orbiting the objective and x2 Navy A-7 Corsair II strike aircraft will be on standby in case heavy enemy resistance is encountered.

Service and Support

Move to the main terminal of the Point Salines International Airport to resupply and procure additional litters.

Command and Control

The Ground Force Commander is the team leader, callsign "Chaos 1-6," from the SMU. The 75th Infantry Regiment (Ranger) headquarters element is located at the Point Salines International Airport's main terminal.

FIGURE 4. MAP OF KEY MILITARY OBJECTIVES

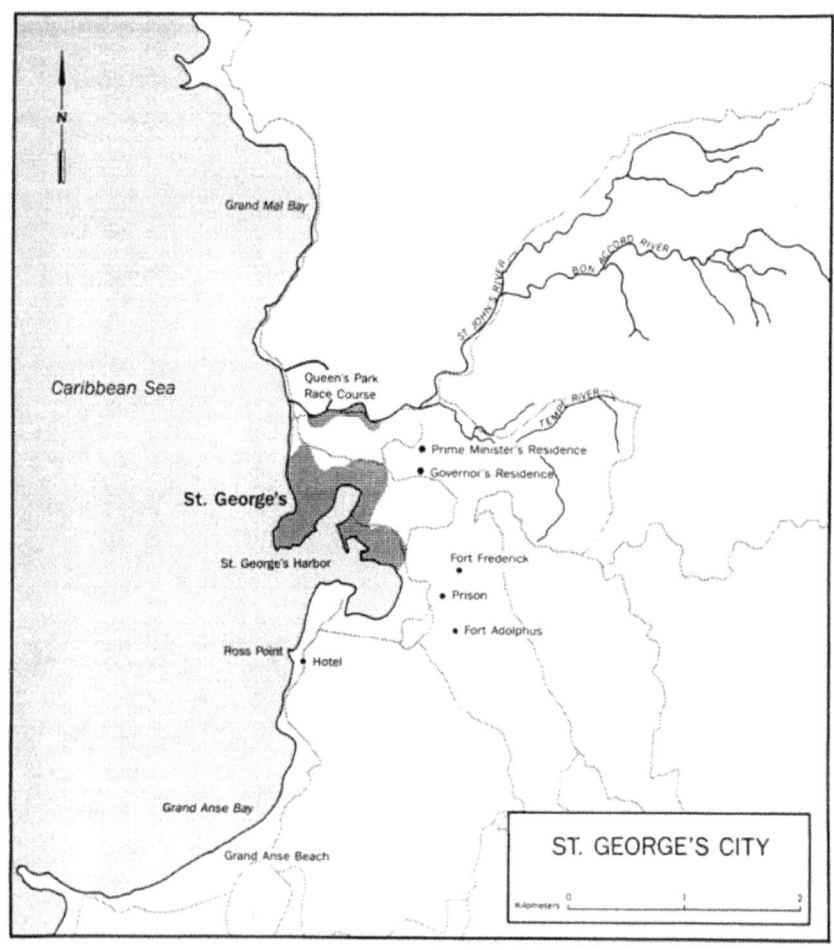

FACT SHEET: TASK FORCE 160

○　　　　　○

United States Army
Instructional Product

The U.S. Army's 160th Aviation Battalion, known as Task Force 160, is an elite group of pilots, aircrew, and maintainers that operate modified helicopters to enable special operations missions. Formed in 1981, this highly selective unit draws from the most experienced aviators in the Army and is trained and resourced to maintain peak proficiency.

Members of Task Force 160 are specially selected and undergo a rigorous assessment process. They regularly train with members of the Special Forces Groups, Ranger Battalions, and Special Missions Units to establish close working relationships and refine their combined Tactics, Techniques, and Procedures (TTPs).

AH-6 Little Bird: This light transport / attack helicopter can be used to ferry troops extremely close to the target or to provide accurate close air support.

Left: A Little Bird transports casualties to a ship off the coast of Grenada during Operation Urgent Fury.

Below: Black Hawks reposition to pick up Rangers at Point Salines.

UH-60 Black Hawk: A medium lift helicopter used to ferry troops.

SIGNALS INTERCEPT ONE

National Security Agency
National SIGINT Operations Center
Fort Meade, MD

Intercepted Radio Recording

Date Recorded - October 25, 1983 21:35 Local

Callsigns mentioned:
- "Base Camp" - Task Force HQ
- "Chaos 6" - SMU team leader / Ground Force Commander
- "RF36" - F/1/75 Ranger platoon leader
- "Warrior 5-1" - Navy VA-87 flight lead

```
1                   :Radio Transmission Begins:

2    [Chaos 6]   Base Camp, Chaos, radio check, over.
```

3	[Base Camp]	Chaos, Base Camp, we read you lima charlie, over.
4	[RF36]	Chaos, 3-6, radio check, over.
5	[Chaos 6]	3-6, Chaos, I have you lima charlie, over.
6	[RF36]	Isolation set. No movement observed, over.
7	[Chaos 6]	Base Camp, Chaos. Isolation set, commencing assault.

Doors appear heavily barricaded...from the outside. Prepping to explosively breach.

Net call, breach is set. I have control. 3, 2, 1, execute, execute, execute![explosion sound]

| 8 | [RF36] | Warrior 5-1, Romeo Foxtrot 3-6, maintain a high orbit over the hospital and let us know if you see any armor trying to sneak up on us, over. |

9	[Warrior 5-1]	Romeo Foxtrot 3-6, Warrior 5-1, roger, out.
10		:Radio Silence; 2 minutes:
11	[Chaos 6]	Troops in contact! [shooting sounds]
12	[RF36]	Chaos, 3-6, we just grabbed that guy who ran out the breach, over.
13	[Chaos 6]	Copy. We're taking casualties in here. They're bum-rushing us! [Screaming and shooting sounds]
14	[RF36]	Roger. Do you want me to flex you a squad for support, over?
15	[Chaos 6]	They're not going down! [Screaming and shooting sounds] They're ripping us apart!
16	[RF36]	Roger, we're coming! Hold on!
17	[Chaos 6]	Negative! 3-6, do not come in here. We'll hold them back. Blow this place.
18	[RF36]	Chaos, say again?

19	[Chaos 6]	3-6, strike this building. Now! Do not let these…*things* escape.
20	[RF36]	Copy. [Muffled shooting sounds] Warrior 5-1, engage the target building. All Foxtrot 3 elements, push out the perimeter. Bombs inbound.
21	[Warrior 5-1]	Foxtrot 3-6, Warrior 5-1 copies. Rolling in.
22		:Radio Silence; 90 Seconds:
23	[Warrior 5-1]	Ordnance delivered. We're winchester.[18] Returning to base.
24	[Base Camp]	Chaos, Base Camp, request sitrep, over.
25		:Radio Silence; 1 minute:
26	[Base Camp]	Chaos, Base Camp, request sitrep, over.
27	[RF36]	Base Camp, Romeo Foxtrot 3-6. Chaos is KIA, all of them. Objective building is destroyed. One male

---

[18] The multiservice tactical brevity code "Winchester" means that the aircraft has no more ordnance to deliver.

recovered but everyone else in there
is gone, over.

28   [Base   Copy. Birds inbound to PZ. Get the
      Camp]   PC out now.[19] Recovery operations
                 will be tasked to another unit,
                 over.

29   [RF36]   Base Camp, Romeo Foxtrot 3-6 copies.
                 Out.

30   :Radio Transmission Ends:

---

[19] PC is an acronym for the term "precious cargo."

Point Salines Airport as viewed from an inbound aircraft.

Rangers move off the airfield while a C-141 transport plane taxis.

Rangers begin a combat patrol after seizing the airport.

Rangers meeting ADM Metcalf are interrupted by a landing aircraft.

Rescued students cheer and wave as they are escorted to safety.

A Ranger jeep team prepares for another patrol.

Ranger scouts during a pause in the action.

Two American students visit with a Ranger jeep team.

A Ranger poses with his weapon during a lull in the action.

SECTION THREE - CONCLUSION

This section includes evidence that shows the series of events that led to the withdrawal of the Task Force and the destruction of Ronde Island. The investigation's final report is included.

INTERROGATION LOG

Central Intelligence Agency
Office of the Inspector General (OIG)
Langley, VA

Interview Recording

Interview Date: October 31, 1983
Interviewer: Bob Smith, OIG Special Agent
Interviewee: Christopher Seward

	:Transcript Begins:
Agent Smith	Please state your name and occupation.
Mr. Seward	Christopher Seward. Assistant VP of the Research Division in Grenada for Essex A&P.

Agent Smith	When did you first become aware of the outbreak on Rhonde Island?
Mr. Seward	Shouldn't I have a lawyer available to me? Or do you Yanks not practice what you preach?
Agent Smith	Mr. Seward, you are not in a position of great leverage. It appears that your company, and perhaps even you specifically, have caused the deaths of numerous people and are potentially criminally and civilly liable. Luckily for you, we are not a law enforcement organization. We are a truth-seeking organization.

Now, when did you first become aware of the outbreak? |
| Mr. Seward | Our people at the facility started getting sick in late September. We couldn't figure out why (throat clearing), but we suspected it was some tainted produce brought in by the locals and served in our cafeteria. |
| Agent Smith | What were the initial symptoms? |

Mr. Seward	Hmm, common flu-like symptoms. Nausea, headache, fever, chills, etcetera. After a couple weeks is when it'd turn and get nasty.
Agent Smith	Describe what you mean by "nasty."
Mr. Seward	You know, they'd turn into raving lunatics who tried to eat you.
Agent Smith	I don't know that. Please provide more detail.
Mr. Seward	(Sighs) They began to hallucinate. They couldn't or wouldn't sleep and suffered from insomnia. They stopped eating and began picking at themselves. We had to restrain them, but the strange thing is they'd get stronger and stronger. We had to add employees to the infirmary staff because it just got too overwhelming. Eventually, the infected would stop speaking and communicating at all and just try to bite and claw anyone close to them.
Agent Smith	Why didn't you notify anyone or ask for help?
Mr. Seward	(Scoffs) Well as you know, the country was preoccupied with a coup. Regardless, the Grenadian health care system wouldn't have been helpful. Rhonde Island was a world-class

	research facility staffed by highly credentialed doctors and scientists. Some believed we could handle it on our own... Yes, they were mistaken in that belief.
Agent Smith	Did you observe any patterns in those who became infected?
Mr. Seward	It affected anyone, local or ex-pat. Sex, age, fitness... didn't matter. The driver for infection was the concentration of exposure to whatever the original source was.
Agent Smith	So, to your knowledge, the illness wasn't communicable between people?
Mr. Seward	Correct, we never observed person-to-person spread.
Agent Smith	When did it get out of control?
Mr. Seward	A week before you Americans invaded, we had an incident where three staff members were killed. We decided to quarantine the remaining sick in the infirmary and overflow areas and abandon the island.
Agent Smith	How many were sick by that time?

Mr. Seward	Out of the total staff of 60, 43 were seriously ill, three were dead, and just 14 of us were left to barricade them in and evacuate to the main island.
Agent Smith	Where does David Pottinger factor into your numbers?
Mr. Seward	Mr. Pottinger abandoned his post like a coward. I hope wherever he is, he is suffering. This is really all his fault if you trace it back.
Agent Smith	Do you know who shot him?
Mr. Seward	...I...I don't know what you're talking about. If he was shot, that is news to me.
Agent Smith	How did you all end up at the hospital near Fort Frederick?
Mr. Seward	When we made landfall, we were promptly captured by the PRA and escorted to the fort. It seemed the leadership there was interested in using us as hostages and human shields. We raised concerns when we explained what happened at the research facility, and they decided to lock us in a nearby hospital.

Agent Smith	Explain what happened when U.S. forces entered the hospital.
Mr. Seward	I knew some of us were sick (begins weeping). I begged the guards to let the healthy ones like me out, but they wouldn't listen. One person was even shot trying to escape. After four days, 12 more of us had turned. The guards barricaded us in and shot at anybody trying to get out. The healthy ones congregated at one end of the hospital and tried to fight the infected ones off, but eventually it was just me. I locked myself in a radiology closet and just waited for them to break in and kill me. Next thing I know, I hear and feel a tremendous blast from the other end of the building. All the infected ones ran towards the noise, and I started hearing shooting and screaming. I decided this was my only chance, and I ran through the melee and out the open entrance. The soldiers inside were fighting off three to a man, but their bullets just weren't doing anything. I ran right into the barrels of the soldiers outside. They tackled and dragged me away just as I heard jets fly past and the hospital blow up (Quiet weeping).

Agent Smith	Why do you think you weren't infected, Mr. Seward?
Mr. Seward	The healthy ones were all off-island the previous month. That's the only reason. I was in London taking meetings when the infection started.
Agent Smith	Ok, that'll do for now...actually, one more thing. As I said, somebody shot at David Pottinger as he tried to escape the facility. Any idea who that was?
Mr. Seward	Uh, no...um, to be honest I barely knew the man. It was a very hectic scene. Could have been anyone. I'm more focused on strategic things, you know. How the facility operates day-to-day is delegated to someone or another.
Agent Smith	I see. Well, we can pause now. Thank you.
	:Transcript Ends:

FRAGMENTARY ORDER TWO

Department of the Army
1st Battalion, 75th Infantry Regiment (Ranger)
Hunter Army Airfield, GA

25 October 1983

Situation

3rd Platoon, F Company (3F) reports that an unknown hostile force destroyed the SMU team they were supporting. Information gathered from a civilian survivor on the objective leads them to believe additional enemy forces associated with the encountered group are assembling at the Essex A&P research facility located on Rhonde Island.

Mission

O/o 3F will assault and clear through the Rhonde Island research facility.

Execution

Commander's Intent

3F will move to Rhonde Island and reconnoiter the area for additional enemy forces. If they are identified and hostile intent is observed, 3F is ordered to destroy the enemy garrison. Endstate: All enemy forces are killed or captured, and intelligence on this force is collected.

Concept of the Operation
- Move to the U.S. Coast Guard Cutter (USCGC) *Chase* via two (2) MH-60 Blackhawks
- Travel to the vicinity of Rhonde Island
- Infiltrate the island via the two (2) RHIB crewed by the cutter[20]
- Assault and clear through the research facility
- Transfer any noncombatants to the USCGC *Chase* for advanced medical care

---

[20] A "RHIB" is a rigid-hulled inflatable boat common on medium and large U.S. military vessels.

- Transfer any captured combatants to the Point Salines airport detention facility

Fire support will be available from x1 AC-130 orbiting the objective and x2 Navy A-6 Intruder strike aircraft will be on standby in case heavy enemy resistance is encountered.

Service and Support

Move to the USCGC *Chase* to resupply.

Command and Control

The Ground Force Commander is the 3F Platoon Leader, callsign "RF36." The 75th Infantry Regiment (Ranger) headquarters element is located at the Point Salines International Airport main terminal.

FIGURE 5. HAND DRAWN MAP OF RESEARCH FACILITY

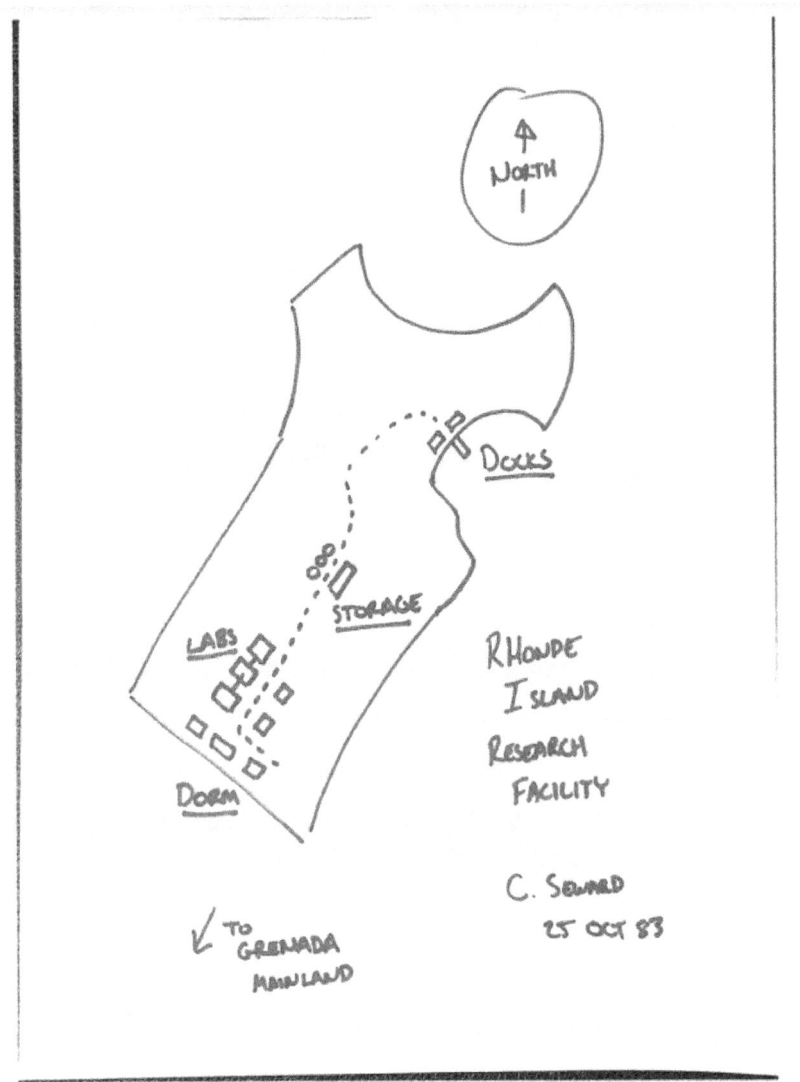

FACT SHEET: AC-130 GUNSHIP

○   ○

United States Air Force
Instructional Product

The AC-130 gunship is a heavily armed, long-endurance, ground-attack variant of the C-130 Hercules fixed-wing transport aircraft. It carries a wide array of ground-attack weapons that are integrated with sophisticated sensors, navigation, and fire-control systems. The airframe is manufactured by Lockheed Martin and Boeing is responsible for the conversion into a gunship.

AC-130 showing 105mm howitzer, 40mm cannons, and minigun barrels.

Close air support roles include supporting ground troops, escorting convoys, and urban operations. Air-interdiction missions are conducted against planned targets and targets of opportunity. Force-protection missions include defending air bases and other facilities.

WITNESS STATEMENT TWO

SWORN STATEMENT
For use of this form, see AR 190-45.

LOCATION	DATE (YYYMMDD)	TIME	FILE NUMBER
USA	19831031	1000	

LAST NAME, FIRST NAME, MIDDLE NAME	GRADE/STATUS
McClelland, Derrick, NMN	E-7 / RA

ORGANIZATION OR ADDRESS

3rd PLT, F Co., 1/75 INF REG (Ranger), Hunter Army Airfield, GA

I, SFC Derrick McClelland , WANT TO MAKE THE FOLLOWING STATEMENT UNDER OATH:

During the invasion of Grenada, I was a Ranger Platoon

Sergeant that observed and engaged infected individuals

associated with the outbreak at the Essex A&P research facility.

After the incident at the hospital near Fort Frederick, we debriefed the civilian we pulled off target. He indicated that a large group of the hostiles were congregated on Rhonde Island, a smaller island about 20 miles off the northern coast of Grenada. We passed this information up to higher headquarters and word came down to go investigate. We were picked up and flown to the Coast Guard cutter Chase off the coast of St. George's. We began to refit and form a hasty plan for infiltrating the island while we transited. The goal was to collect intelligence first, which is why we didn't land via helicopter directly at the facility. We didn't know what we'd be up against.

The civilian told us that the main campus was on the southern end of Rhonde Island and that was where most of the hostiles were likely to congregate. We decided our best course of action was to insert by two RHIBs aboard the cutter to the docks located on the north end of Rhonde Island. Taking the docks on the less populated part of the island would give us a foothold with structures for defense and efficient disembarkation.

By now, it was late into the night with limited illumination. While we transited to Rhonde Island on the cutter, the AC-130 gunship was already orbiting the facility and passing back that they were not picking up any signatures on their FLIR. We began to assume that the hostiles had departed the island and either made it to the mainland to engage U.S. forces or may have even evacuated to another country to escape. We reported this to higher, and they had us continue mission to recon what may have been left behind.

When we reached the launch point, half the platoon boarded the RHIBs and headed for the docks. The PL would accompany the first chalk and establish the foothold.[21] Then, the RHIBs would cycle back and pick up the rest of the platoon. The first

---

[21] The "PL," or platoon leader is the officer-in-charge of the 30 soldier unit.

wave encountered no resistance and so the full platoon inserted at the docks and formed a perimeter.[22]

We left the Coasties behind at the dock to defend our exfil, and we made our way south along the only road. I use the word "road" loosely as it actually wasn't much more than a golf cart path. The plan was to patrol south along the road until we entered the valley that runs straight down the middle of the island running north-to-south. At that point, our weapons squad and sniper elements moved to the high ground to the southeast and set up to overwatch the rest of the platoon's movement.

Our next waypoint along the pathway was a storage and maintenance area. We cleared through until we reached a large warehouse. When we entered the warehouse we encountered a lone figure squatting over another. He had his back to us. When we told him to put his hands up, he turned around and was gnawing at the detached arm of the other person. He screamed

---

[22] To "infil," or infiltrate, means to enter the objective area. To "exfil," or exfiltrate, means to leave the objective area.

and started running towards us, and we opened up on him. He didn't die. He was shredded from our rounds and could only crawl, but he was intent on getting to us. I walked over to him and put one in his head with my pistol. That did the trick.

We knew for sure that we were dealing with something supernatural now. We'd all seen the "Night of the Living Dead" and "Dawn of the Dead" movies, and there was no question this was what we were seeing.[23] I had to calm the boys down because fighting zombies was not something we'd trained for. That helped some but I was just as spooked as they were.

Doc Holme looked at the zombie and confirmed that the body was somehow working at ambient temperature. We assumed this is why the gunship wasn't seeing them move around. The state of the other bodies in the warehouse led us to believe that, unlike the movies, getting bit didn't turn you into one of them. You had to have been infected some other way. I said a silent prayer for

---

[23] The original versions of these two movies debuted in 1968 and 1978, respectively.

them and that we wouldn't be exposed to whatever that thing might be.

With the area cleared, we picked back up our bounding overwatch and the weapons squad displaced to their second OP.[24] They observed multiple zombies milling about the research campus. With the overwatch set, we moved to the first set of buildings closest to us, which turned out to be the laboratories.

That's where the fight really picked up.

INITIALS OF PERSON MAKING STATEMENT	PAGE
DM	3 OF 3

DA FORM 2814, DEC 1979

---

[24] "OP" stands for observation post.

INTERVIEW TRANSCRIPT TWO

Department of the Army
Office of the Deputy Chief of Staff for Intelligence G-2
Washington, DC

Interview Recording Transcript - Session 2
Interview Date: 31 OCT 1983
Interviewer: Major Simon Conner, Counterintelligence Section
Interviewee: PFC Geoff Holme, 1/75th Rangers

	:Transcript Begins:
MAJ Conner	What happened once you all reached the main campus?
PFC Holme	We began to clear the buildings closest to us, which ended up being the laboratories.
MAJ Conner	Did you take contact in there?

PFC Holme	Not at first. The labs were three, two-story buildings connected by enclosed walkways. The northernmost building, the first one, was mostly storage, supplies, and administrative areas.
MAJ Conner	And the infected outside hadn't noticed you all yet?
PFC Holme	No, sir. 1st and 3rd squads were silently clearing the buildings. 2nd squad was on the outside isolating the laboratories, but they hadn't yet engaged anyone. They were just observing and reporting at that time.
MAJ Conner	Do you remember who made that call?
PFC Holme	The platoon sergeant, Sergeant McClelland, made the recommendation to Lieutenant Shepherd. He said that we needed to maintain our advantage as long as possible and secure a foothold in one of the buildings. Shepherd agreed.
MAJ Conner	Okay, continue.
PFC Holme	In the second building, we came across a serious looking scientific workspace with an

inner and outer door, kind of like a spaceship's airlock that you'd see in the movies. We got in there and found the only survivor.

He was an older guy named Paul. He said he was the head researcher there and figured out that some experiment of theirs had tainted the island's drinking water. He asked us if we'd drank anything and only visibly calmed down when we reassured him we hadn't.

He explained that when the infected started escaping the infirmary, he saw a group of people running to the dorms for safety. He made a break for the hardened lab room instead. Once inside, he was able to make a cure or something that neutralized the tainted water's effect on himself.

Sergeant McClelland asked him if he knew of any other survivors. Paul told us there was a large safe room in the dorms rated for hurricanes, and people could have taken shelter in there. McClelland passed the info to Lieutenant Shepherd, and they were talking

	through the plan when the 1st squad guys made contact with a group of zombies inside Lab Building #3.
MAJ Conner	Did that finally kick the hornet's nest?
PFC Holme	Yes, sir. It was a shit show after that. The 1st squad guys put down the zombies inside and passed the word that only head shots would knock them down for good. The zombies outside heard the commotion and started running towards Lab Building #3. 2nd squad was just outside and began engaging them. I looked out the window and could see the zombies coming at us, getting ripped to shreds by body shots. Limbs and chunks were coming off of them, and they'd fall down but would then crawl instead.
MAJ Conner	Why not just make the head shots?
PFC Holme	Sir, no offense, but have you been in combat?
MAJ Conner	No, I haven't.

PFC Holme	Well, I know you've qualified on your rifle at a minimum. You know the Army trains for body shots, center-mass on a stationary target. Instead, try a moving target and add in the effects of all the adrenaline that comes from literal monsters coming at you. It's not as easy as it looks. The boys did a great job, though. Once the zombies got close enough, they were able to put them down for good.
MAJ Conner	Makes sense to me. What happens next?
PFC Holme	Shepherd gave the word that we had to get to the dorm and confirm that there were no survivors in the safe room. He told the overwatch element to shoot any targets in the open ahead of our advance. I felt 100% better once the boys on the hill started shooting with the sniper rifles. The noise split the attention of the zombies, and we were able to bound from building-to-building, clearing and cleaning up any individual zombies.
MAJ Conner	Had you all taken any casualties up to that point?

PFC Holme	Yes. Guys had been bit and clawed but nobody had been killed in the movement up to the dorm. Paul told us that the sickness wasn't transferable through human-to-human contact, so I just patched up some deep gashes here-and-there and kept moving.
MAJ Conner	Does anything unusual happen leading up to entering the dorm?
PFC Holme	Other than fighting zombies, sir? No, it was pretty standard stuff.
MAJ Conner	Fair enough. Please continue.
PFC Holme	The rest of the buildings were relatively small. One story buildings with few internal rooms, so breaching the main entrance pretty much cleared the space. We would leapfrog from building-to-building until we were at the dorm. And by then, between us and the overwatch, we'd put down all the zombies that were milling around outside.
MAJ Conner	Could the infected open doors?
PFC Holme	Good question. No, sir. They seemed to lack the coordination to do so. After the fact, we

	guessed that they were trapped in whatever building or room that they had succumbed to the sickness. That would explain why everything went wrong at the dorm.
MAJ Conner	I know this part is tough to talk about. Do you need a break first?
PFC Holme	(Sniffs) No, sir. I'd like to get this over with.
MAJ Conner	Okay, Holme. What happens in the dorm?
PFC Holme	1st squad sets up containment on the outside and 2nd and 3rd squads go into the dorm to clear. I go in with the platoon sergeant and Paul, the researcher. We didn't have anywhere to stash him while we cleared, so Sergeant McClelland told me to keep an eye on him. It also turned out that many buildings had internal rooms with keypad door locks and Paul knew all the combinations. We breached the dorm, and there were a lot of zombies in there. It makes sense now because that's where the sick would have been put to convalesce.

	We had our first Ranger killed there – from 2nd squad. They entered a room and a zombie just jumped him from behind and ripped his throat out. It was horrific. At the same time, the 3rd squad stumbles into the infirmary where there were a ton of zombies. They get bum rushed and start taking casualties. In the mass confusion of managing our KIA and 3rd squad getting jumped, Paul decided to slip away and check the safe room for survivors. I saw him just as he unlocked the door. I screamed at him to stop, but it was too late. The door pushed open, and he was swallowed by a horde of zombies. The survivors in there didn't have the benefit of Paul's treatment, so of course they had all succumbed to the outbreak.
MAJ Conner	At this point, are you all outnumbered?
PFC Holme	Yes, absolutely. The zombies had the advantage of numbers, speed, and we're really low on ammo now.

	McClelland called "landslide" on the radio and ordered everyone out of the dormitory.[25] We just hauled ass out of there. There were just too many of them, and we had no chance. Sir, it was a horror movie. I'll never be able to forget what I saw there.
MAJ Conner	How did you personally escape?
PFC Holme	McClelland was following 3rd squad out of the building when one of the zombies grabbed him. I bum-rushed them both and pushed McClelland out of an open window just behind them. We both fell onto a stack of old pallets below the window and left the zombie screaming at us above.
MAJ Conner	So the infected were just chasing you all out of the dormitory?
PFC Holme	Yes, they were pouring out of our breach point. The 1st squad guys were firing and helping the injured get away, but there were just too

---

[25] In this context, the radio call "landslide" is an order to abandon the target as quickly as possible.

	many and we were moving too slow. We were about 50 meters from the dormitory when Lieutenant Shepherd had us get on-line to make a stand and face the horde. We were all standing there in the open, waiting for the zombies to crash into us like a wave, when the most beautiful sound I've ever heard happened.
MAJ Conner	What was it?
PFC Holme	The sound of the support-by-fire...[26]

---

[26] A "support-by-fire" is the overwatch force that covers the maneuver elements, typically with heavy machine guns, rockets, mortars, and sniper fire.

SIGNALS INTERCEPT TWO

National Security Agency
National SIGINT Operations Center
Fort Meade, MD

Intercepted Radio Recording

Date Recorded - October 26, 1983 04:30 Local Time

Callsigns mentioned:
- "RF36" - F/1/75 Ranger platoon leader
- "RF34" - F/1/75 Ranger weapons squad leader

1   :Radio Transmission Begins:

2   [RF36] (Screaming and shooting in
             background) 4, this is 6, we're
             getting overrun. Need you to
             cover our exfil from the dorm.

3   [RF34]   Roger, 6. You all need to get
               in line with the southernmost
               lab building for us to have
               clear fields of fire.

4   [RF36]   (Screaming and shooting in
               background) Roger,
               understood…we aren't going to
               make it that far.

5   [RF34]   Okay, standby and get low!
               We're going to be right over
               your heads.

6   :Radio Transmission Ends:

INTERVIEW TRANSCRIPT THREE

Department of the Army
Office of the Deputy Chief of Staff for Intelligence G-2
Washington, DC

Interview Recording Transcript - Session 3
Interview Date: 31 OCT 1983
Interviewer: Major Simon Conner, Counterintelligence Section
Interviewee: PFC Geoff Holme, 1/75th Rangers

PFC Holme	Let me tell you, if they had that sound on cassette tape, I'd buy it today. The PL had us all go prone to the ground, and we watched the weapons squad guys rip them to shreds. All three guns went to a cyclic rate of fire shooting right over us and into the crowd of

	zombies.[27] It was so close that the PL's radio took a round. The sound and flashes were enough to capture the zombie horde's attention, and they started moving up the hill towards the overwatch element. We took that opportunity to start bounding back towards the road in the direction of our exfil.
MAJ Conner	Is this when the gunship comes on station?
PFC Holme	It had been there all along, but we couldn't use it while clearing or inside the buildings. All these zombies were now out in the open. The PL needed to call in a fire mission but had no communications. Shepherd dashed into one of the lab buildings on our way out of the research campus, grabbed a telephone on a random desk, and made a call to the Salines Airport Main Terminal...and someone actually picked up!

---

[27] A cyclic rate of fire is a sustained rate of fire whereby the gunner pulls the trigger and only ceases when the belt of ammunition is complete.

	He yelled something into the receiver, and we just booked it out of there. Man, I would have loved to have heard the other end of *that* conversation! Anyways, we're bounding back north when the gunship overhead starts going to work too. Let me tell you, it came online just in time! The rounds started ripping into the zombies and covering our exfil. We alternated with the weapons guys, overwatching and engaging while the gunship gave us some breathing room. This finally kept the horde off of us. We eventually linked up with them at the dock and scrambled onto the waiting RHIBs that the Coast Guard guys had warmed up for us.
MAJ Conner	Who made the call to level the island?
PFC Holme	Once we were back aboard the cutter, I was busy patching up our guys, so I don't know. I heard that Lieutenant Shepherd got on the radio with headquarters and convinced them that the place needed to be demolished.

	We were steaming south towards the mainland when I heard the Navy come overhead and start to make their runs on the island. Have you ever heard of an "Alpha Strike," sir?
MAJ Conner	No, what is that?
PFC Holme	It's when an aircraft carrier sends all of its aircraft on an attack mission. I'll never forget standing on the deck of that boat, a postcard perfect Caribbean sunrise in the background, while wave-after-wave of jets streaked in to bomb the island…
	:Recording Ends:

FLASH TRAFFIC

○   ○

United States Navy
Commander, Carrier Air Wing Six (CVW-6)
USS Independence CV-62

291936Z OCT 83
FM COMSECONDFLT NORFOLK VA//NN//
TO USS INDEPENDENCE CV-62//OO//
INFO CNO WASHINGTON DC//NN//

BT
TOP SECRET//N02300//
MSGID/FLASH/CNO//
SUBJ/**ALPHA STRIKE TARGET RHONDE ISLAND**//
REF/A/MSG/COMSECONDFLT NORFOLK VA/201311OCT83//
REF/B/DOC/CNO/20OCT83//
NARR/**ENTIRETY OF RHONDE ISLAND GRENADA IS TO BE
NAPALMED IMMEDIATELY. EXPEND ALL ORDINANCE. REDUCE
ALL STRUCTURES.**//
POC/CAPT. DOOR/-/DSN 228-0547/-N311B/202-262-0547//

FACT SHEET: CARRIER AIR WING SIX

United States Navy
Instructional Product

During Operation Urgent Fury, Carrier Air Wing Six (CVW-6) embarked on the USS Independence (CV-62), a Forrestal-class supercarrier. Independence had a total crew of just over 5,000 sailors including the ship's company, air wing crew, flag staff, and Marines. With a displacement of 61,000 tons, a length over 1,000 feet long, and a range of 15,000 kilometers; the carrier was a massive floating airport.

The air wing consisted of a variety of aircraft that could be used to build a tailored response package based on the needs of the mission. The squadrons and aircraft aboard CVW-6 included:

- Fighter Squadron 32 (VF-32); 14 F-14A Tomcat
- Fighter Squadron 14 (VF-14); 13 F-14A Tomcat
- Attack Squadron 176 (VA-176); 16 A-6E Intruder

- Attack Squadron 87 (VA-87); 12 A-7E Corsair
- Attack Squadron 15 (VA-15); 12 A-7E Corsair
- Airborne Early Warning Squadron 122 (VAW-122); 4 E-2C Hawkeye
- Tactical Electronic Warfare Squadron 131 (VAQ-131); 4 EA-6B Prowler
- Helicopter Anti-submarine Squadron 15 (HS-15); 6 SH-3H Sea King
- Air Anti-submarine Squadron 28 (VS-28); 10 S-3A Viking
- Carrier Onboard Delivery; 1 C-1A Tracker

A-7E Corsair Attack Aircraft

A-6 Intruder Attack Aircraft

FINAL EVALUATION

O   O

Central Intelligence Agency
Office of the Inspector General (OIG)
Langley, VA

October 1984

Memorandum For: President of the United States (POTUS),
                    Ronald Reagan

Via: Director of Central Intelligence (DCI),
                    William J. Casey

Subject: Results of investigation into Operation
                    Urgent Fury paranormal incident

1. CIA-OIG has determined that the hostile action associated with the Essex A&P corporation on Rhode Island was the result of an industrial accident.

2. Based on 1) the statements of the confirmed head researcher of the Essex A&P corporation at the originating facility, and 2) documentation collected from the corporate office in the capital St. George's: A chemical spill of the substances Tetrodotoxin and Datura was exacerbated by extreme rainfall associated with a tropical depression. This in turn tainted the water supply of the research facility and caused the adverse symptoms in the staff present on the island.

3. Based on the testimony of an Essex A&P executive that was interrogated by CIA-OIG: All infected staff members that made landfall on the Grenadian mainland were destroyed during the rescue attempt near Fort Frederick.

4. Based on the statements of the Ranger force sent to reconnoiter the Rhonde Island facility and collect intelligence: No further infection is probable and all infected individuals were relegated to the research facility's footprint.

5. Based on the after action reports from the air strike battle damage assessment: All standing structures were bombed and burned leaving no trace and no surviving infected.

6. It is the opinion of CIA-OIG that this incident was a one-off encounter and there is no active threat of a similar infection incident occurring in the future.

7. CIA-OIG recommends that, under an unrelated justification, chemical and occupational safety regulatory bodies worldwide be notified to increase caution associated with the storage of the named chemicals.

8. As Essex A&P Ltd. and its staff are a predominantly United Kingdom-based organization, consistent with existing information sharing agreements, CIA has forwarded all evidence and analyses to relevant British security services for action.

DISCLOSURE RISK ASSESSMENT

O   O

Central Intelligence Agency
Office of the Inspector General (OIG)
Langley, VA

October 1984

Name	CPT Theodore Shepherd
Current Residence	Fort Bragg, NC
Disclosure Risk Score	LOW
Evaluator's Notes	Shepherd is eager to join the Agency after completing his service commitment. We assess that he hopes this incident will serve as a stepping stone for his career, and he will not jeopardize the opportunity.

	Recommend he be recruited into the Agency, even if only for a support position.

*****

Name	1SG Derrick McClelland
Current Residence	Fort Benning, GA
Disclosure Risk Score	MODERATE
Evaluator's Notes	McClelland displays clear disgruntlement with how the incident was managed. He mourns for his lost Rangers and is in a highly emotional state. Reminders of criminal penalties for disclosure and loss of retirement benefits gave him pause. We assess that he is currently agitated, but his strong moral values will deter him from disclosing publically. Recommend he be monitored under the domestic surveillance program for five (5) years and then reassessed.

Name	Mr. Geoff Holme
Current Residence	Los Angeles, CA
Disclosure Risk Score	HIGH
Evaluator's Notes	Holme is highly distraught and withdrawn. We do not observe indications of substance abuse, however his general behaviors put him at a high probability of onset addiction. It appears he wants to forget about the incident completely, however there is no way to determine at present if he is prone to unauthorized disclosure. Recommend he be monitored under the domestic surveillance program for ten (10) years and then reassessed.

*****

Name	Mr. Christopher Seward
Current Residence	London, United Kingdom

Disclosure Risk Score	LOW
Evaluator's Notes	Seward is now residing in the U.K. and is still employed by Essex A&P. He has been promoted to a Senior Vice President role and is now one of the top most compensated executives at the organization. We assess that the company is fearful of their liability in the incident and Seward's promotion to be their way of placating and controlling him. Since the incident, he has likely signed additional nondisclosure agreements tied to these monetary benefits and is highly unlikely to break them. Recommend no surveillance and to prioritize assets elsewhere.

*****

Name	Miscellaneous Rangers and supporting servicemembers
Current Residence	Various

Disclosure Risk Score	LOW
Evaluator's Notes	The remaining Rangers are relatively junior and sufficiently leery of the military justice system. While they were in direct contact with the hostile force, they were not privy to the overall picture of the operation and are now limited in what they have to disclose.
	Aircrew were not briefed on the hostile force and did not make direct contact.
	Recommend no additional surveillance for these individuals.

NEWSPAPER ARTICLE

Intercontinental Daily News

Search Continues For Missing British Corporation Staff in Grenada

By Madeline Fezell | September 1984

Nearly one year after the U.S. led intervention in Grenada, the Essex Agricultural & Petrochemical Ltd corporation is still seeking answers to what happened to their Grenada-based employees.

After a coup attempt left communist sympathizers in control of the island nation, foreign combatants from Cuba began to flood the country prompting the massive military response from the United States and Caribbean allies. The American hostages, mostly students and staff of the St. George's Medical College, were rescued to great fanfare. Essex A&P staff did not fare as well.

"We are deeply concerned for the safety of our missing brothers and sisters," stated Essex A&P executive Christopher Seward. "We continue to use the full might and influence of our organization to resolve this matter. We call upon all the governments involved to disclose what they know and help us bring peace to our treasured family and friends."

When asked about Grenada during a recent gala benefiting a London charity, the Foreign Secretary commented, "we continue to make diplomatic overtures to the Soviet Union and Cuban governments, but to date we have made no progress in understanding the current status of our citizens or what involvement those countries had in their disappearance."

Families are growing increasingly frustrated with the response, especially after seeing how much effort was expended to rescue American citizens. They feel too little has been done to investigate the matter and suspect foul-play by the communist forces on the island.

"There is currently a £100,000 reward for any information leading to the whereabouts of our cherished staff. Please contact us, no tip is too small. You never know what good could happen with even the smallest bit of information." stated Seward.

This page left blank intentionally

TELEPHONE INTERCEPT TWO

National Security Agency
National SIGINT Operations Center
Fort Meade, MD

Intercepted Telephone Recording

Date Recorded - October 26, 1983 04:56 Local Time

Callers:
- 1LT Theodore Shepherd - F/1/75 Ranger platoon leader
- AMN Adam Bollinger - Air Force logistics plans specialist

Location:
- Originating: Rhonde Island, Grenada
- Receiving: Passenger Terminal, Point Salines Airport

1   :Telephone Line Ringing:

2   [Bollinger]   Uh, hello?

3   [Shepherd]   (Heavy gunfire in the background) This is Lieutenant Shepherd with the Rangers, who is this?

4   [Bollinger]   Uh, Airman Bollinger with the airlift wing, sir. I'm not really supposed to-

5   [Shepherd]   Listen, Bollinger. You hear that!? (More heavy gunfire in the background) I'm in a pinch and I need you to relay a message for me.

6   [Bollinger]   Is, uh…this a joke?

7   [Shepherd]   Bollinger, I don't have time to explain this to you! You got a pen and paper handy?

8   [Bollinger]   Sure, uhhh. Just one second.

9   [Shepherd]   (Even more heavy gunfire in the background) Bollinger!

10   [Bollinger]   I'm here, sir! Okay, I'm ready to copy.

11	[Shepherd]	Get over to the Tactical Operations Center and tell them that the Rangers on Rhonde Island need gunship support immediately. Tell them we don't have comms and they won't be able to see the enemy forces on FLIR because...because...ah, just tell them that we need them to fire for effect with everything they have, danger close to the south of our position. We're bounding north. Tell them they're cleared hot. You got that!?
12	[Bollinger]	Okie-dokey, I will tell the operations center that you're-
13	[Shepherd]	No time for a read back. Danger close to our SOUTH! Gotta run!
14		(Phone receiver clattering; yelling and gunfire in the background)
15	[Bollinger]	Uh, hello? Lieutenant? Sir?
16		:Telephone Line Disconnected:

This page left blank intentionally

REFERENCE NOTES & CREDITS

This is a work of fiction, however painstaking efforts have been exerted to ensure that the storytelling intertwines with the actual events of the conflict from the timeline, key personalities, the weather forecast, and much more.

Internet search engines (like Google) and online encyclopedias (like Wikipedia) were efficient resources for the initial research. Every effort has been made to drill down to the source material from those sites, and others, to provide due credit as noted on that site. Not every citation is directly relevant to this composition.

Any omission is unintentional and we welcome feedback that helps correct any mistakes.

Operation Urgent Fury

1. Clarke, Jeffrey J. *Operation Urgent Fury: Invasion of Grenada, October* (PDF). United States Army. Archived (PDF) from the original on 24 September 2015. Retrieved 21 August 2015.
2. Cole, Ronald (1997). "Operation Urgent Fury: The Planning and Execution of Joint Operations in Grenada" (PDF). Archived from the original (PDF) on 16 November 2011. Retrieved 9 November 2006.
3. "Medals Outnumber G.I.'s in Grenada Assault". *The New York Times*. 30 March 1984. Archived from the original on 13 February 2017. Retrieved 9 February 2017.
4. Clodfelter, Micheal (2017). *Warfare and Armed Conflicts: A Statistical Encyclopedia of Casualty and Other Figures, 1492–2015* (4th ed.). McFarland. p. 645. ISBN 978-0786474707.
5. "Study Faults U.S. Military Tactics in Grenada Invasion". *The Washington Post*. Archived from the original on 2 July 2019. Retrieved 2 July 2019.
6. "The Invasion of Grenada". PBS.org. Archived from the original on 20 March 2017. Retrieved 27 August 2017.
7. Russell, Lee; Mendez, Albert (2012). *Grenada 1983*. London: Osprey Publishing. p. 45.
8. "Soldiers During the Invasion of Grenada". CardCow Vintage Postcards. Archived from the original on 8 December 2015. Retrieved 9 October 2015.
9. Kukielski, Phil (18 September 2013). "How Grenada reshaped the US military". *The Boston Globe*. Archived from the original on 2 August 2020. Retrieved 25 April 2020.
10. Seabury, Paul; McDougall, Walter A., eds. (1984). *The Grenada Papers*. San Francisco: Institute for Contemporary Studies. ISBN 0-917616-68-5. OCLC 11233840.
11. Scoon, Sir Paul (2003). *Survival for Service: My Experiences as Governor General of Grenada*. Oxford: Macmillan Caribbean. pp. 136, 145. ISBN 0-333-97064-0. OCLC 54489557.
12. Moore, Charles (2015). "Chapter 5: Reagan plays her false". *Margaret Thatcher: The Authorized Biography, Volume Two: Everything She Wants*. Great Britain: Allen Lane, Penguin Books. p. 119. ISBN 978-0-713-99288-5. OCLC 922929186. OL 27339067M. pp. 118–119.
13. "Caribbean Islands – A Regional Security System". country-data.com. Archived from the original on 26 April 2017. Retrieved 18 November 2008.
14. Moore, Charles (2016). *Margaret Thatcher: At her Zenith*. p. 130.

15. "United Nations General Assembly resolution 38/7". United Nations. 2 November 1983. Archived from the original on 10 August 2018. Retrieved 5 March 2016.

16. Kukielski, Philip (2019). *The U.S. Invasion of Grenada: legacy of a flawed victory*. Jefferson, NC: McFarland & Company. pp. 213–214. ISBN 978-1-4766-7879-5. OCLC 1123182247.

17. Burrowes, Reynold A. (1988). *Revolution and rescue in Grenada: an account of the U.S.–Caribbean invasion*. New York: Greenwood Press. ISBN 0-313-26066-4. OCLC 17943224.

18. Murphy, Philip (2013), *Monarchy and the End of Empire*, Oxford: Oxford University Press, p. 169, ISBN 978-0-19-921423-5, retrieved 28 April 2023

19. Payne, Anthony (1984). *Grenada : revolution and invasion*. Sutton, Paul K., Thorndike, Tony. New York: St. Martin's Press. p. 31. ISBN 0-312-35042-2. OCLC 10548141.

20. Peter Collier, David Horowitz (January 1987). "Another 'Low Dishonest Decade' on the Left". *Commentary*.

21. Gailey, Phil; Warren Weaver Jr. (26 March 1983). "Grenada". *The New York Times*. Retrieved 11 March 2008.

22. Burrowes, Reynold A. (1988). *Revolution and Rescue in Grenada: An Account of the U.S.-Caribbean Invasion*. Greenwood Press. p. 63. ISBN 978-0-313-26066-7. Archived from the original on 19 October 2021. Retrieved 25 March 2021.

23. Sir Paul Scoon, G-G of Grenada, at 2:36 on YouTube

24. Martin, Douglas (9 September 2013). "Paul Scoon, Who Invited Grenada Invaders, Dies at 78". *The New York Times*. Archived from the original on 2 April 2019. Retrieved 9 February 2017.

25. Thatcher, Margaret (2011). *The Downing Street Years*. London: HarperCollins. p. 841. ISBN 9780062029102.

26. "Paul Scoon; had key role in invasion of Grenada". *BostonGlobe.com*. Archived from the original on 27 September 2017. Retrieved 27 September 2017.

27. Martin, Douglas (8 September 2013). "Paul Scoon, Who Invited Grenada Invaders, Dies at 78". *The New York Times*. Archived from the original on 2 April 2019. Retrieved 9 February 2017.

28. "Assembly calls for cessation of 'armed intervention' in Grenada". *UN Chronicle*. 1984. Archived from the original on 27 June 2007.

29. "United Nations General Assembly resolution 38/7". United Nations. 2 November 1983. Archived from the original on 19 November 2000.

30. Carter, Gercine (26 September 2010). "Ex-airport boss recalls Cubana crash". *Nation Newspaper*. Archived from the original on 24 January 2012. Retrieved 16 October 2011.

31. Cozier, Tony (12 March 1985). "Barbados Prime Minister Dies Of Heart Attack". Associated Press. Retrieved 7 February 2023.

32. Kukielski, Phil (8 September 2013). "How Grenada reshaped the US military". *The Boston Globe*. Archived from the original on 2 August 2020. Retrieved 25 April 2020.

33. Harding, Steve (1984). *Air War Grenada*. Missoula, Montana: Pictorial Histories Publishing Company. pp. 8–9. ISBN 9780933126527.

34. Huchthausen, Peter (2004). *America's Splendid Little Wars: A Short History of U.S. Engagements from the Fall of Saigon to Baghdad*. New York: Penguin. p. 69. ISBN 978-0-14-200465-4.

35. *Grenada 1983* by Lee E. Russell and M. Albert Mendez, 1985 Osprey Publishing Ltd., ISBN 0-85045-583-9 pp. 28–48.

36. Dominguez, Jorge (1 January 1989). *To Make a World Safe for Revolution: Cuba's Foreign Policy*. Center for International Affairs. pp. 154–253. ISBN 978-0674893252.

37. Domínguez, Jorge I. (1989). *To Make a World Safe for Revolution: Cuba's Foreign Policy*. Cambridge, Massachusetts: Harvard University Press. ISBN 0-674-89325-5. pp. 168–169

38. Gleijeses, Piero (2002). *Conflicting Missions: Havana, Washington and Africa, 1959–1976*. Chapel Hill, NC: University of North Carolina Press. p. 256. ISBN 978-0-807-82647-8.

39. Woodward, Bob (1987). *Veil: The Secret Wars of the CIA 1981–1987*. Simon & Schuster. ISBN 9780671601171.

40. Leckie, Robert (1998). *The Wars of America*. Castle Books. ISBN 9780785809142.

41. "A Caribbean Arms Cache". *Engineer*. Fort Leonard Wood, Missouri: United States Army Engineer School. 13 (4): 31. December 1983.

42. Timeline – World History Documentaries (22 April 2017). "A Close Look At History's Great Military Blunders | Politics By Other Means". Archived from the original on 28 November 2021. Retrieved 7 February 2023 – via YouTube.

43. "A Grenada SEAL widow tells her story | San Diego Reader". *www.sandiegoreader.com*. Archived from the original on 9 July 2020. Retrieved 8 July 2020.

44. "SEAL History: Navy SEALs in Grenada Operation Urgent Fury". Navy SEAL Museum. Archived from the original on 16 March 2017. Retrieved 6 April 2016.

45. Stuart, Richard W. (2008). *Operation Urgent Fury: The Invasion of Grenada, October 1983* (PDF). U.S. Army. Archived (PDF) from the original on 24 September 2015. Retrieved 21 August 2015.

46. Kreisher, Otto. "Operation Urgent Fury – Grenada". Marine Corps Association & Foundation. Archived from the original on 19 April 2016. Retrieved 6 April 2016.

47. "Caron (DD-970)". *public2.nhhcaws.local*. Retrieved 26 December 2019.

48. "SEAL History: Navy SEALs in Grenada Operation Urgent Fury". *Navy Seal Museum*. National Navy UDT-SEAL Museum. Archived from the original on 16 March 2017. Retrieved 7 August 2021.

49. Kukielski, Philip (2019). *The U.S. Invasion of Grenada : legacy of a flawed victory*. Jefferson, North Carolina: McFarland & Company. pp. 66–68. ISBN 978-1-4766-7879-5. OCLC 1123182247.

50. "Turning the Tide: Operation Urgent Fury". *Combat Reform*. Archived from the original on 7 April 2016. Retrieved 6 April 2016.

51. Kreisher, Otto (October 2003). "Operation Urgent Fury – Grenada". *Marine Corps Association and Foundation*. Archived from the original on 19 April 2016. Retrieved 28 April 2016.

52. Wayne Tommell, Anthony (1986). "Soviet Vehicle in Collection Thanks to 2d AAV Bn" (PDF). *Fortitudine*. Vol. 15, no. 4. p. 21. Retrieved 25 March 2023.

53. Smith, Hedrick; Times, Special To the New York (15 November 1983). "U.S. DEFENDING GRENADA ACTION BEFORE O.A.S." *The New York Times*. ISSN 0362-4331. Retrieved 7 February 2023.

54. Karas, John M.; Goodman, Jerald M. (1984). "The United States Action in Grenada: An Exercise in Realpolitik". *University of Miami Inter-American Law Review*. 16 (1): 53–108.

55. Robert j, Beck (2008). "Grenada". *Max Planck Encyclopedias of International Law*. Max Planck Institute for Comparative Public Law and International. doi:10.1093/law:epil/9780199231690/e1292. ISBN 978-0-19-923169-0. Archived from the original on 2 October 2018. Retrieved 7 February 2023 – via Oxford Public International Law.

56. Waters, Maurice (1986). "The Invasion of Grenada, 1983 and the Collapse of Legal Norms". *Journal of Peace Research*. 23 (3): 229–246. doi:10.1177/002234338602300303. JSTOR 423822. S2CID 143082909.

57. Chayes, Abram (15 November 1983). "GRENADA WAS ILLEGALLY INVADED". *The New York Times*. Opinion. ISSN 0362-4331. Retrieved 7 February 2023.

58. Zunes, Stephen (October 2003). "The U.S. Invasion of Grenada: A Twenty Year Retrospective". Foreign Policy in Focus. Archived from the original on 13 July 2008. Retrieved 12 July 2008.

59. "United Nations Security Council vetoes". United Nations. 28 October 1983. Archived from the original on 28 June 2017. Retrieved 28 June 2017.

60. Magnuson, Ed (21 November 1983). "Getting Back to Normal". *Time*. Archived from the original on 14 February 2008.

61. "Nightline | Vanderbilt Television News Archive". *tvnews.vanderbilt.edu*. Archived from the original on 18 April 2021. Retrieved 19 October 2021.

62. "Vanderbilt Television News Archive". *tvnews.vanderbilt.edu*. Archived from the original on 18 April 2021. Retrieved 19 October 2021.

63. "Vermonters at Washington March". *Rutland Herald*. 14 November 1983. p. 20. Archived from the original on 7 December 2020 – via Newspapers.com.

64. *United Nations Yearbook*, Volume 37, 1983, Department of Public Information, United Nations, New York

65. "Spartacus Educational". Archived from the original on 29 June 2008.

66. "Reagan: Vote loss in U.N. 'didn't upset my breakfast'". *The Spokesman-Review*. 4 November 1983. Retrieved 30 June 2013.

67. "Thatcher letter to Reagan ("deeply disturbed" at U.S. plans) [memoirs extract]". Margaret Thatcher Foundation. 25 October 1983. Archived from the original on 27 December 2008. Retrieved 25 October 2008.

68. Thatcher, Margaret (1993) *The Downing Street Years* p. 331.

69. Tran, Mark (10 November 2014). "Reagan apologised to angry Thatcher over Grenada, tapes reveal". *The Guardian*. Archived from the original on 12 November 2020. Retrieved 8 November 2020.

70. John Campbell, *Margaret Thatcher Volume Two: The Iron Lady* (2011) pp. 273–279.

71. Gary Williams, "'A Matter of Regret': Britain, the 1983 Grenada Crisis, and the Special Relationship", *Twentieth Century British History* 12#2 (2001): 208–230.

72. "St. Vincent's Prime Minister to officiate at renaming of Grenada international airport". Caribbean Net News newspaper. 26 May 2009.

73. "Bishop's Honour: Grenada airport renamed after ex-PM". Caribbean News Agency (CANA). 30 May 2009. Archived from the original on 12 June 2009.

74. "Prime Minister Speech at Airport Renaming Ceremony". *Grenadian Connection*. 30 May 2009. Archived from the original on 21 November 2016. Retrieved 21 November 2016.

75. Kukielski, Philip (2019). *The U.S. Invasion of Grenada : legacy of a flawed victory*.

Jefferson, North Carolina: McFarland & Company. p. 46. ISBN 978-1-4766-7879-5. OCLC 1123182247.

76. Sandler, Norman D. (28 May 1984). "Reagan's view of Vietnam War unwavering". *United Press International*. Archived from the original on 2 August 2020. Retrieved 22 January 2020.

77. Beinart, Peter (7 June 2010). "Think Again: Ronald Reagan". *Foreign Policy*. Archived from the original on 30 March 2020. Retrieved 22 January 2020.

78. Chen, Edwin; Richter, Paul (2 March 1991). "U.S. Shakes Off Torment of Vietnam". *Los Angeles Times*. Archived from the original on 1 August 2020. Retrieved 22 January 2020.

79. Clines, Francis X. (13 December 1983). "Military of U.S. 'Standing Tall,' Reagan Asserts". *The New York Times*. Archived from the original on 29 March 2020. Retrieved 22 January 2020.

80. Spector, Ronald (1987). "U.S. Marines in Grenada 1983" (PDF). p. 6. Archived (PDF) from the original on 4 July 2013. Retrieved 6 April 2013.

81. Naylor, Sean (2015). *Relentless Strike, the Secret History of Joint Special Operations Command*. St. Martin's Press. ISBN 978-1-250-01454-2.

75th Ranger Regiment

1. Neville, Leigh (2015), *Special Forces in the War on Terror*, General Military, Osprey Publishing, ISBN 978-1472807908, OCLC 889735079.

2. Urban, Mark (2012). *Task Force Black: The Explosive True Story of the Secret Special Forces War in Iraq* (1st ed.). New York: St. Martin's Griffin. ISBN 978-1-250-00696-7. OCLC 759914001. Retrieved 11 October 2022.

3. Garland, Albert N.; Smyth, Howard McGaw (1965). *U.S. Army in World War II – Mediterranean Theater of Operations – Sicily and the Surrender of Italy* (PDF). Washington, D.C.: United States Government Printing Office. Archived from the original (PDF) on 27 September 2012.

4. "USSOCOM Fact Book – 2017" (PDF). USSOCOM. 2017. pp. 19–20. Archived (PDF) from the original on 27 April 2017. Retrieved 27 March 2017.

5. SPECIAL OPERATIONS FORCES Opportunities Exist to Improve Transparency of Funding and Assess Potential to Lessen Some Deployments. GAO-15-571 (PDF) (Report). Government Accountability Office. July 2015. Archived (PDF) from the original on 22 March 2016. Retrieved 2 June 2016.

6. Naylor, Sean (2015). "Chapter 4". *Relentless Strike : The Secret History of Joint Special Operations Command* (1st ed.). New York: St. Martin's Press. ISBN 978-1-250-01454-2. OCLC 908554550.

7. *Special Operations Forces Reference Manual* (Fourth ed.). MacDill AFB, Florida: Joint Special Operations University. June 2015. pp. 78–82. ISBN 9781933749914. Archived from the original on 28 March 2017. Retrieved 27 March 2017.

8. "Mission – 75th Ranger Regiment". *GoArmy*. 23 July 2015. Archived from the original on 12 February 2017. Retrieved 27 March 2017.

9. Atlamazoglou, Stavros (23 December 2021). "ARMY RANGERS HAVE BEEN DEPLOYED TO COMBAT FOR 7,000 DAYS STRAIGHT". *Sandboxx*. Archived from the original on 1 October 2022.

10. "Biography of Captain Church". *Ranger Hall of Fame*. United States Army. Archived from the original on 8 April 2005.

11. "History & Heritage". *Army.mil*. Archived from the original on 12 July 2011. Retrieved 12 October 2022.

12. Ankony, Robert (Summer 2015). "They Saw Us First" (PDF). *Patrolling*. Vol. 28, no. 2. 75th Ranger Regiment Association, Inc. pp. 2, 43–48. Archived from the original (PDF) on 11 October 2022.

13. Ranger Training Brigade (February 2011). *Ranger Handbook SH 21-76* (PDF). US Army Ranger School. Archived from the original (PDF) on 3 October 2022.

14. Finlayson, Kenneth; Jones Jr., Robert W. (2006). "Rangers in World War II: Part I—The Formation and Early Days" (PDF). *Veritas*. Vol. 2, no. 3. USASOC. pp. 64–70. ISSN 1553-9830. PB 31-05-2. Archived from the original (PDF) on 20 August 2021. Retrieved 11 October 2022.

15. Zimmerman, Dwight Jon (29 September 2016). "Col. William O. Darby The Ranger Who Led the Way". *Defense Media Network*. Archived from the original on 22 September 2021. Retrieved 11 October 2022.

16. S&D (Fall 2004). "The 1st Ranger Battalion" (PDF). *Patrolling*. Vol. 19, no. 2. 75th Ranger Regiment Association, Inc. pp. 61–62. Archived from the original (PDF) on 11 October 2022.

17. Bahmanyar, Mir. "Darby's Rangers". *MirBahmanyar*. Archived from the original on 11 October 2022. Retrieved 11 October 2022.

18. Hogan Jr., David W. (1992). *US Army Special Operations In World War II CMH 70-42* (PDF). United States Army Center of Military History. OCLC 22909690. Archived from the original (PDF) on 28 July 2022. Retrieved 11 October 2022.

19. Garland & Smyth 1965.

20. Black, Robert W. (2009). *The Ranger Force : Darby's Rangers in World War II*. Stackpole Books. pp. 146–154. ISBN 9780811743839.

21. Garland & Smyth 1965, p. 226-230.

22. "Interview with Private Harry Perlmutter, Part I". Special Operations History Foundation. Archived from the original on 2 July 2013. Retrieved 19 July 2013.

23. Finlayson, Kenneth; Jones Jr., Robert W. (2007). "RANGERS IN WORLD WAR II Part II, Sicily and Italy". *Veritas*. Vol. 3, no. 1. USASOC. ISSN 1553-9830. Archived from the original on 24 October 2020. Retrieved 11 October 2022.

24. "Lineage and Honors 75th RANGER REGIMENT". *United States Army Center of Military History*. 27 April 2017. Archived from the original on 21 July 2022. Retrieved 11 October 2022.

25. Lehman, Milton (15 June 1946). "The Rangers Fought Ahead of Everybody". *The Saturday Evening Post*. Vol. 218, no. 50. pp. 28-29, 45, 48, 50, 52.

26. Lomell, Leonard; Kuhn, Jack (12 June 2006). "D-DAY: INTERVIEW WITH TWO U.S. 2ND RANGER BATTALION MEMBERS WHO DESCRIBE THE ATTACK AT POINTE-DU-HOC" (Interview). Interviewed by Frederick, Michael; Masci, Joseph F. Archived from the original on 7 June 2022 – via History.net.

27. Caraccilo, Dominic J. (2015). *Forging a Special Operations Force : the US Army Rangers*. Solihull, West Midlands: Helion & Company. p. 28. ISBN 978-1-910777-36-7.

28. "2014 Ammunition Hall of Fame Inductee MAJOR GENERAL (RET.) JOHN C. RAAEN, JR" (PDF). *Joint Chiefs of Staff*. 2014. Archived from the original (PDF) on 9 August 2022. Retrieved 11 October 2022.

29. Jones Jr., Robert W. (2009). "FROM OMAHA BEACH TO THE RHINE The 5th Ranger Battalion in the European Theater" (PDF). *Veritas*. Vol. 5, no. 2. USASOC. ISSN 1553-9830. Archived from the original (PDF) on 6 June 2022. Retrieved 11 October 2022.

30. Krivdo, Michael E. (2018). "RESCUE AT CABANATUAN" (PDF). *Veritas*. Vol. 14, no. 2. USASOC. ISSN 1553-9830. Archived from the original (PDF) on 30 January 2022. Retrieved 11 October 2022.

31. Strausbaugh, Leo V. "The 6th Ranger Battalion". Descendants of World War II Rangers. Archived from the original on 29 December 2015. Retrieved 15 February 2017.

32. "Unit History 75TH RANGER REGIMENT". *Army.mil*. Archived from the original on 24 March 2021. Retrieved 11 October 2022.

33. *75th Ranger Regiment Heritage*. GoArmy.com. Archived from the original on 11 May 2017.

34. Stanton, Shelby L. (1993). *Rangers at War : Combat Recon in Vietnam* (1st ed.). New York: Ivy Books. pp. 8–9. ISBN 978-0-8041-0875-1. OCLC 28093451.

35. Black, Robert W. (June–July 2010). "Rangers in Korea". *VFW [magazine]*. VFW. pp. 42–43. ISSN 0161-8598. Archived from the original on 11 October 2022.

36. Ankony, Robert C. (2009). *LURPS: A Ranger's Diary of Tet, Khe Sanh, A Shau, and Quang Tri* (Revised ed.). Lanham, MD: Hamilton Books. ISBN 978-0761843726. OCLC 266915908.

37. Gebhardt, James F. (2005). *Eyes Behind the Lines: US Army Long-Range Reconnaissance and Surveillance Units* (PDF). Combat Studies Institute Press, Army University Press. pp. 45–110. ISBN 978-1-4289-1633-3. Archived from the original (PDF) on 11 October 2022.

38. Meadows, Mark R. (12 October 2012). Long-Range Surveillance Unit Force Structure in Force XXI [thesis] (PDF) (Report). Fort Leavenworth, KS: US Army Command and General Staff College. Archived from the original (PDF) on 11 October 2022.

39. Kolb, Richard K. (August 2012). "Last Days of the Infantry in Vietnam, 1972". *VFW [magazine]*. VFW. pp. 36–42. ISSN 0161-8598. Archived from the original on 11 October 2022.

40. "Lineage and Honors 1st BATTALION, 75th RANGER REGIMENT". *United States Army Center of Military History*. 27 April 2017. Archived from the original on 21 July 2022. Retrieved 11 October 2022.

41. "Lineage and Honors 2d BATTALION, 75th RANGER REGIMENT". *United States Army Center of Military History*. 27 April 2017. Archived from the original on 21 July 2022. Retrieved 11 October 2022.

42. "Lineage and Honors 3D BATTALION, 75TH RANGER REGIMENT". *United States Army Center of Military History*. 28 January 2015. Archived from the original on 12 August 2022. Retrieved 11 October 2022.

43. Murphy, Jack (22 June 2013). "Evolution of the 75th Ranger Regiment: RRD". *TheNewsRep*. Archived from the original on 13 November 2018. Retrieved 13 November 2018.

44. "75th Ranger Regiment Special Troops Battalion". *USASOC*. Archived from the original on 1 October 2022. Retrieved 11 October 2022.
45. "Lineage and Honors SPECIAL TROOPS BATTALION 75TH RANGER REGIMENT". *United States Army Center of Military History*. 26 March 2013. Archived from the original on 21 July 2022. Retrieved 11 October 2022.
46. "75th Rangers - Living the legacy". USASOC. 26 October 2009. Archived from the original on 11 October 2022. Retrieved 11 October 2022.
47. Dickstein, Corey (19 March 2012). "Hunter-based Army Rangers awarded for actions in Afghanistan". *Savannah Morning News*. Archived from the original on 23 May 2014. Retrieved 26 March 2012.
48. Myers, Meghann (18 January 2018). "This woman will be the first to join the Army's elite 75th Ranger Regiment". *Army Times*. Archived from the original on 29 August 2022.
49. Finkel, Gal Perl (21 March 2017). "WIN THE CLOSE FIGHT". *The Jerusalem Post*. Archived from the original on 22 March 2017.
50. Janofsky, Michael (23 October 2001). "A NATION CHALLENGED: THE EARLY CASUALTIES; 2 Soldiers Remembered for Their Focus and Patriotism". *The New York Times*. Archived from the original on 2 February 2017. Retrieved 17 March 2017.
51. Neville 2015, p. 29.
52. Cawthorne, Nigel (2008). *The Mammoth Book of Inside the Elite Forces*. London: Robinson Publishing. ISBN 978-1845298210. OCLC 176894746.
53. Bailey, Tracy A. (5 May 2015). "1st Battalion, 75th Ranger Regiment honors its heroes". Army.mil. Archived from the original on 25 August 2016.
54. Lamothe, Dan (1 September 2015). "Six little-known stories about secretive Joint Special Operations Command, as told in a new book". *The Washington Post*. Archived from the original on 22 August 2016.
55. Neville, Leigh (2016). *US Army Rangers 1989–2015: Panama to Afghanistan*. Oxford: Osprey Publishing. ISBN 978-1-4728-1540-8. OCLC 951712359.
56. "2 Most Wanted Al Qaeda Leaders in Iraq Killed by U.S., Iraqi Forces". *Fox News*. 19 April 2010. Archived from the original on 1 July 2015. Contribution from Associated Press
57. Ibrahim, Waleed (19 April 2010). "Al Qaeda's top two leaders in Iraq have been killed". *Reuters*. Archived from the original on 24 September 2015.
58. Jaffe, Greg; Ryan, Missy (26 January 2016). "The U.S. was supposed to leave Afghanistan by 2017. Now it might take decades". *The Washington Post*. Archived from the original on 3 June 2016.
59. Cooper, Helene (27 April 2017). "'Friendly Fire' May Have Killed 2 U.S. Soldiers in Afghanistan Raid". *The New York Times*. Archived from the original on 29 April 2017.
60. Myers, Meghann; deGrandpre, Andrew (28 April 2017). "Army Rangers killed in Afghanistan were possible victims of friendly fire". *Army Times*. Archived from the original on 25 August 2021.
61. "Afghanistan IS head killed in raid – US and Afghan officials". BBC. 8 May 2017. Archived from the original on 23 May 2017.
62. Starr, Barbara (8 March 2017). "US Marines join local forces fighting in Raqqa". *CNN*. Archived from the original on 10 March 2017.
63. "75th Ranger Regiment About". *Fort Benning*. Archived from the original on 2 September 2022. Retrieved 23 August 2020.

64. "Lineage and Honors MILITARY INTELLIGENCE BATTALION 75st RANGER REGIMENT". *United States Army Center of Military History*. 7 October 2020. Archived from the original on 21 July 2022. Retrieved 11 October 2022.

65. Keller, Jared (30 October 2020). "US special operations forces behind al-Baghdadi raid awarded Presidential Unit Citation". Task & Purpose. Archived from the original on 9 July 2022. Retrieved 21 May 2021.

66. "Join the 75th Ranger Regiment". *Fort Benning*. Archived from the original on 19 April 2022. Retrieved 7 October 2019.

67. "Army Ranger Qualifications". Army.com. 14 March 2014. Archived from the original on 26 June 2014. Retrieved 14 July 2014.

68. "Join the Rangers". GoArmy.com. Archived from the original on 5 May 2013.

69. "Training". GoArmy.com. Archived from the original on 27 April 2011. Retrieved 26 May 2017.

70. "RASP 1&2". GoArmy.com. Archived from the original on 5 May 2013. Retrieved 26 May 2017.

71. Ankony, Robert C. (Fall 2015). "H/75 - E/52 LRP - 1ST CAV LRRP" (PDF). *Patrolling*. Vol. 28, no. 3. 75th Ranger Regiment Association, Inc. p. 32. Archived from the original (PDF) on 11 October 2022.

72. "The Big 5". *Fort Benning*. Archived from the original on 2 March 2013. Retrieved 28 April 2018.

73. Tanner, Lindsey (15 August 2011). "Do-it-yourself battlefield medicine saves lives". *NBCNews*. Associated Press. Archived from the original on 26 February 2022.

74. Bowden, Mark (1999). *Black Hawk Down: A Story of Modern War*. Berkeley, CA: Atlantic Monthly Press. p. 8. ISBN 978-0-87113-738-8.

75. U.S. Army Ranger Association (2011). "Ranger Hall of Fame". U.S. Army Ranger Association, Inc. Archived from the original on 23 December 2010. Retrieved 19 March 2011.

76. Lock, John D. (2005). *The Coveted Black and Gold : A Daily Journey Through the U.S. Army Ranger School Experience* (2nd ed.). Tucson, AZ: Fenestra Books. p. 219. ISBN 978-1-58736-367-2. OCLC 57965974.

77. "Rangers protest black beret decision". *USA Today*. Associated Press. 19 June 2001. Archived from the original on 27 March 2022.

78. Bahmanyar, Mir (2011). *Shadow Warriors: A History of the US Army Rangers*. Osprey Publishing. ISBN 978-1-78096-075-3. OCLC 1021807447.

79. "DA Approves Ranger's New Headgear". *Army.mil*. Archived from the original on 1 October 2014. Retrieved 21 November 2012.

80. "Adopting the Beret". *Pentagram [newspaper]*. Army News Service. 23 March 2001. Archived from the original on 27 December 2013. Retrieved 21 November 2012.

81. Siter, Bridgett (3 August 2001). "Private Ceremony". *Stripe*. Army News Service. Archived from the original on 27 December 2013. Retrieved 21 November 2012.

82. "Guide to the Wear and Appearance of Army Uniforms and Insignia PAM 670-1" (PDF). Department of the Army. 26 January 2021. Archived from the original (PDF) on 25 September 2022. Retrieved 11 January 2022.

83. Adkin, Mark (1989). *Urgent Fury : The Battle for Grenada*. Lexington, MA: Lexington Books. p. 195. ISBN 9780669207170. OCLC 18836419.

84. "Congressional Veterans Caucus: Jason Crow". *Military Times*. Archived from the original on 28 January 2022. Retrieved 15 January 2021.
85. Martinez, Luis; Caron, Christine (25 October 2011). "Army Ranger Dies On 14th Deployment". ABC. Archived from the original on 27 March 2022. Retrieved 25 January 2021. Sgt. 1st Class Kristoffer Domeij served in Iraq and Afghanistan.
86. Dreazen, Yochi J. (25 October 2011). "For Elite U.S. Troops, War's End Will Only Mean More Fighting". *The Atlantic*. Archived from the original on 27 March 2022. Retrieved 23 January 2021.

Zombie

1. Maçek III, J. C. (15 June 2012). "The Zombification Family Tree: Legacy of the Living Dead". *PopMatters*. Archived from the original on 3 June 2020.
2. Deborah Christie, Sarah Juliet Lauro, ed. (2011). *Better Off Dead: The Evolution of the Zombie as Post-Human*. Fordham University Press. p. 169. ISBN 978-0-8232-3447-9.
3. "Zombie", in Oxford English Dictionary Online, accessed 23 May 2014.
4. Peter Laws, *The Frighteners: Why We Love Monsters, Ghosts, Death & Gore*, Icon Books, 2018
5. Doris L Garraway, *The Libertine Colony: Creolization in the Early French Caribbean*, Duke University Press, 2005
6. Pereira Do Nascimento, Jose (1903). *Diccionario Portuguez-Kimbundu*. Huilla: Typographia da Missão.
7. de Assis Junior, A. *Diccionario Portuguez-Kimbundu*. Luanda Argente, Santos.
8. Deborah Christie, Sarah Juliet Lauro, ed. (2011). Better Off Dead: The Evolution of the Zombie as Post-Human. Fordham University Press. p. 169. ISBN 0-8232-3447-9, 9780823234479.
9. Stokes, Jasie (17 March 2010). *Ghouls, Hell and Transcendence: The Zombie in Popular Culture from 'Night of the Living Dead' to 'Shaun of the Dead'* (Master's thesis). Brigham Young University. Retrieved 3 February 2016.
10. Savage, Annaliza (15 June 2010). "'Godfather of the Dead' George A. Romero Talks Zombies". *Wired*. Retrieved 2 October 2011.
11. Szanter, Ashley; Richards, Jessica K. (24 August 2017). *Romancing the Zombie: Essays on the Undead as Significant 'Other'*. McFarland. ISBN 9781476667423.
12. McGlotten, Shaka; Jones, Steve (26 August 2014). *Zombies and Sexuality: Essays on Desire and the Living Dead*. McFarland. ISBN 9780786479078.
13. George, Sam; Hughes, Bill (1 November 2015). *Open Graves, Open Minds: Representations of vampires and the Undead from the Enlightenment to the present day*. Oxford University Press. ISBN 9781526102157.
14. Moreman, Christopher M.; Rushton, Cory James (10 October 2011). *Zombies Are Us: Essays on the Humanity of the Walking Dead*. McFarland. ISBN 9780786488087.
15. "Zombie". *Oxford English Dictionary*. Oxford University Press. 1998.
16. George A. Romero, *Dawn of the Dead* Archived 8 November 2020 at the Wayback Machine (Working draft 1977), horrorlair.com.
17. JLSVT - George Romero on YouTube.

18. McAlister, Elizabeth (1995). "A Sorcerer's Bottle: The Visual Art of Magic in Haiti". In Cosentino, Donald J. (ed.). *Sacred Arts of Haitian Vodou*. Los Angeles, California: UCLA Fowler Museum of Cultural History. pp. 304–321. ISBN 978-0930741471.
19. Asante, Molefi Kete; Mazama, Ama (2009). *Encyclopedia of African Religion*. SAGE. ISBN 978-1-4129-3636-1.
20. Daniels, Kyrah Malika (1 January 2021). "Vodou harmonizes the head-pot, or, Haiti's multi-soul complex". *Religion*. 52 (3): 9. ISSN 0048-721X.
21. Davis, Wade (1997). *The Serpent and the Rainbow*. New York City: Simon & Schuster. p. 186. ISBN 978-0684839295.
22. Wilentz, Amy (26 October 2012). "A Zombie Is a Slave Forever". *The New York Times*. Haiti. Retrieved 31 October 2012.
23. Wilentz, Amy (December 2011). "Response to "I Walked with a Zombie"". *amywilentz.com*. Retrieved 2 February 2018.
24. Pané, Fray Ramón. "The relación of Fray Ramón Pane *[sic]*". *faculty.smu.edu*. Archived from the original on 13 April 2021.
25. Whitehead, Neal L. (2011). *Of Cannibals and Kings: Primal Anthropology in the Americas*. Penn State Press. pp. 39–41.
26. Edmonds, Ennis B.; Gonzalez, Michelle A. (2010). *Caribbean Religious History: An Introduction*. NYU Press. p. 111.
27. Seabrook, William (1929). *The Magic Island*. Blue Ribbon Books. p. 103.
28. "Code pénal". *www.oas.org*. Retrieved 12 March 2018.
29. Mars, Louis P. (1945). "Media life zombies for the world". *Man*. 45 (22): 38–40. doi:10.2307/2792947. JSTOR 2792947.
30. Hurston, Zora Neale (1984) [1942]. *Dust Tracks on a Road* (2nd (1942) ed.). Urbana, IL: University of Illinois Press. p. 205).
31. Moreman, Christopher M.; Rushton, Cory James (2011). *Race, Oppression and the Zombie: Essays on Cross-Cultural Appropriations of the Caribbean Tradition*. McFarland. p. 3. ISBN 978-0-7864-5911-7.
32. Moore, Brian L. (1995). *Cultural Power, Resistance, and Pluralism: Colonial Guyana, 1838–1900*. University of California Press. pp. 147–149.
33. Dayan, Joan (1998). *Haiti, History, and the Gods*. University of California Press. p. 37.
34. Marinovich, Greg; Silva Joao (2000). *The Bang-Bang Club Snapshots from a Hidden War*. William Heinemann. p. 84. ISBN 978-0-434-00733-2.
35. Marinovich, Greg; Silva Joao (2000). *The Bang-Bang Club Snapshots from a Hidden War*. William Heinemann. p. 98. ISBN 978-0-434-00733-2.
36. Niehaus, Isak (June 2005). "Witches and Zombies of the South African Lowveld: Discourse, Accusations and Subjective Reality". *The Journal of the Royal Anthropological Institute*. 11 (2): 197–198. doi:10.1111/j.1467-9655.2005.00232.x.
37. Davis, E. W. (1983). "The ethnobiology of the Haitian zombi". *Journal of Ethnopharmacology*. 9 (1): 85–104. doi:10.1016/0378-8741(83)90029-6. PMID 6668953.
38. Davis, Wade (1985), *The Serpent and the Rainbow*, New York: Simon & Schuster, pp. 92–95.
39. Davis, Wade (1988), *Passage of Darkness: The Ethnobiology of the Haitian Zombie*, University of North Carolina Press, pp. 115–116.

40. Terence Hines (2008). "Zombies and Tetrodotoxin". Skeptical Inquirer (csicop.org). Retrieved 9 March 2018.
41. Booth, W. (1988). "Voodoo Science". *Science*. 240 (4850): 274–277. Bibcode:1988Sci...240..274B. doi:10.1126/science.3353722. PMID 3353722.
42. Oswald, Hans Peter (2009). *Voodoo*. BoD – Books on Demand. p. 39. ISBN 978-3-8370-5904-5.
43. ^ Littlewood, Roland; Chavannes Douyon (11 October 1997). "Clinical findings in three cases of zombification". *The Lancet*. 350 (9084): 1094–1096. doi:10.1016/s0140-6736(97)04449-8. PMID 10213568. S2CID 38898590. Retrieved 28 March 2014.
44. Dein, Simon (January 2006). "Interview with Roland Littlewood on 5th December 2005" (PDF). *World Cultural Psychiatry Research Review*. 1 (1): 57–59. Archived from the original (PDF) on 6 February 2016.
45. Littlewood, Roland (1 December 1997). "The plight of the living dead". *Times Higher Education*. Retrieved 28 March 2014.
46. Pulliam, June Michele; Fonseca, Anthony J. (19 June 2014). *Encyclopedia of the Zombie: The Walking Dead in Popular Culture and Myth: The Walking Dead in Popular Culture and Myth*. ABC-CLIO. pp. 113–. ISBN 9781440803895. Retrieved 10 May 2015.
47. Bishop, Kyle William (26 January 2010). *American Zombie Gothic: The Rise and Fall (and Rise) of the Walking Dead in Popular Culture*. McFarland. pp. 41–. ISBN 9780786455546. Retrieved 10 May 2015.
48. Dalley, Stephanie (1989). *Myths from Mesopotamia: Creation, the Flood, Gilgamesh, and Others*. Oxford, England: Oxford University Press. p. 155. ISBN 978-0-19-283589-5.
49. Dalley, Stephanie (1989). *Myths from Mesopotamia: Creation, the Flood, Gilgamesh, and Others*. Oxford, England: Oxford University Press. p. 80. ISBN 978-0-19-283589-5.
50. "Books: Mumble-Jumble". TIME. 9 September 1940. Archived from the original on 13 October 2007. Retrieved 5 November 2013.
51. Warner, Marina. *A forgotten gem: Das Gespensterbuch ('The Book of Ghosts'), An Introduction*.
52. H. P. Lovecraft, *Supernatural Horror in Literature* (1927, 1933–1935).
53. "When Zombies Attack!". UGO.com. 24 June 2008. Archived from the original on 20 June 2008. Retrieved 5 November 2013.
54. "Miskatonic University library – H.P. Lovecraft in the Comics". Yankeeclassic.com. Retrieved 5 November 2013.
55. Clasen, Mathias (2010). "Vampire Apocalypse: A Biocultural Critique of Richard Matheson's I Am Legend". *Philosophy and Literature*.
56. Biodrowski, Steve. "*Night of the Living Dead*: The classic film that launched the modern zombie genre".
57. Jones, Tanya Carinae Pell (15 April 2014). "From Necromancy to the Necrotrophic: Resident Evil's Influence on the Zombie Origin Shift from Supernatural to Science". In Farghaly, Nadine (ed.). *Unraveling Resident Evil: Essays on the Complex Universe of the Games and Films*. McFarland & Company. pp. 7–18. ISBN 978-0-7864-7291-8.
58. Levin, Josh (19 December 2007). "How did movie zombies get so fast?". Slate.com. Retrieved 5 November 2013.

59. Lodge, Guy (22 May 2021). "Streaming: Army of the Dead and cinema's best zombie films". *The Guardian*. Retrieved 21 February 2022.
60. Chernov, Matthew (21 May 2021). "'Walking Dead' Whiskey to Survival Kits: Gruesome Gift Ideas for Zombie Fans". *Variety*. Retrieved 21 February 2022.
61. "White Zombie (1932) Review". Archived from the original on 12 September 2015.
62. "Zombies, Malls, and the Consumerism Debate: George Romero's Dawn of the Dead".
63. "IMDb: Most Popular "Zombie" Feature Films Released In 2014". *IMDb*.
64. Dendle, Peter (28 August 2012). *The Zombie Movie Encyclopedia, Volume 2: 2000–2010*. McFarland, Incorporated, Publishers. ISBN 9780786461639.
65. Towlson, Jon (29 October 2018). "Why Night of the Living Dead was a big-bang moment for horror movies". *British Film Institute*. Retrieved 27 May 2020.
66. Stephen Harper, *Night of the Living Dead: Reappraising an Undead Classic. Bright Lights Film Journal*, Issue 50, November 2005.
67. Pulliam, June (2007). "The Zombie". In Joshi, S. T. (ed.). *Icons of Horror and the Supernatural*. Westport, Connecticut: Greenwood Press. ISBN 978-0313337802.
68. Twitchell, James B. (1985). *Dreadful Pleasures: An Anatomy of Modern Horror*. Oxford: Oxford University Press. ISBN 978-0195035667.
69. Roger Ebert, review of *Night of the Living Dead*, Chicago *Sun-Times*, 5 January 1969; last accessed 8 July 2014.
70. "Zombies". GreenCine. Archived from the original on 14 July 2014. Retrieved 5 November 2013.
71. Booker, M. Keith (2010). *Encyclopedia of Comic Books and Graphic Novels*. Vol. 1: A–L. ABC-CLIO. p. 662. ISBN 9780313357473.
72. "Re-Animator". Rotten Tomatoes. 18 October 1985. Retrieved 5 November 2013.
73. Newman, Kim (2011). *Nightmare Movies: Horror on Screen Since the 1960s*. A&C Black. p. 559. ISBN 9781408805039.
74. Barber, Nicholas (21 October 2014). "Why are zombies still so popular?". *BBC*. Retrieved 31 May 2019.
75. Hasan, Zaki (10 April 2015). "INTERVIEW: Director Alex Garland on Ex Machina". *HuffPost*. Retrieved 21 June 2018.
76. "12 Killer Facts About Shaun of the Dead". *Mental Floss*. 23 January 2016. Retrieved 31 May 2019.
77. "How '28 Days Later' Changed the Horror Genre". *The Hollywood Reporter*. 29 June 2018. Retrieved 31 May 2019.
78. Kermode, Mark (6 May 2007). "A capital place for panic attacks". London: Guardian News and Media Limited. Retrieved 12 May 2007.
79. "Stylus Magazine's Top 10 Zombie Films of All Time". Archived from the original on 13 November 2018. Retrieved 10 April 2009.
80. Cronin, Brian (3 December 2008). "John Seavey's Storytelling Engines: George Romero's 'Dead' Films". Comic Book Resources. Archived from the original on 6 December 2008. Retrieved 4 December 2008.
81. Levin, Josh (24 March 2004). "Dead Run". Slate. Retrieved 4 December 2008.
82. Reeves, Ben (30 December 2011). "Guinness World Records 2012 Gamer's Edition Preview". *Game Informer*. Retrieved 31 December 2011.

83. Chandni Doulatramani (9 May 2013). "Walking Dead breathes life into AMC results". *Reuters*. Retrieved 19 May 2013.

84. Luckhurst, Roger (2015). *Zombies: A Cultural History*. Reaktion Books. ISBN 9781780235646.

85. Nguyen, Hanh (31 December 2018). "'One Cut of the Dead': A Bootleg of the Japanese Zombie Comedy Mysteriously Appeared on Amazon". *IndieWire*. Retrieved 2 March 2019.

86. "One Cut of the Dead (Kamera o tomeru na!) (2017)". *Rotten Tomatoes*. Retrieved 2 March 2019.

87. Paffenroth, Kim (2006). *Gospel of the Living Dead: George Romero's Visions of Hell on Earth*. Waco: Baylor University Press. ISBN 978-1932792652.

88. Rockoff, Adam (2002). *Going to Pieces: The Rise and Fall of the Slasher Film, 1978–1986*. Jefferson, NC: McFarland. p. 35. ISBN 978-0-7864-1227-3.

89. Clute, John; Grant, John, eds. (1999). "Zombie Movies". *The Encyclopedia of Fantasy*. New York: St. Martin's Press. p. 1048. ISBN 978-0-312-19869-5.

90. Cripps, Charlotte (1 November 2006). "Preview: Max Brooks' Festival of the (Living) Dead! Barbican, London". *The Independent*. Archived from the original on 7 May 2022. Retrieved 19 September 2008.

91. McAlister, Elizabeth (1 January 2012). "Slaves, Cannibals, and Infected Hyper-Whites: The Race and Religion of Zombies". *Anthropological Quarterly*. 85 (2): 457–486. doi:10.1353/anq.2012.0021. ISSN 1534-1518. S2CID 144725423. Archived from the original on 25 September 2015. Retrieved 26 August 2020.

92. Pegg, Simon (4 November 2008). "Simon Pegg on why the undead should never be allowed to run". *The Guardian*. ISSN 0261-3077. Retrieved 15 February 2019.

93. Kenreck, Todd (17 November 2008). "Surviving a zombie apocalypse: 'Left 4 Dead' writer talks about breathing life into zombie genre". *Video game review*. NBC News. Retrieved 3 December 2008.

94. Daily, Patrick. "Max Brooks". *Chicago Reader*. Archived from the original on 21 December 2008. Retrieved 28 October 2008.

95. Craig Wilson, "Zombies lurch into popular culture via books, plays, more", *USA Today*, 9 April 2009, p. 1D (1st page of Life section, above the fold), found at Zombies lurch into popular culture article at USA Today. Retrieved 13 April 2009.

96. Bishop, Kyle William (17 September 2015). *How Zombies Conquered Popular Culture: The Multifarious Walking Dead in the 21st Century*. McFarland. ISBN 9780786495412.

97. Bodart, Joni Richards (10 November 2011). *They Suck, They Bite, They Eat, They Kill: The Psychological Meaning of Supernatural Monsters in Young Adult Fiction*. Scarecrow Press. ISBN 9780810882270.

98. Marowski, Daniel G.; Stine, Jean C. (15 October 1985). *Contemporary literary criticism*. Vol. 35. Gale Research Company. ISBN 9780810344099.

99. Cassiday, Bruce (1 September 1993). *Modern mystery, fantasy, and science fiction writers*. Continuum. ISBN 9780826405739.

100. Jason Thompson (9 January 2014). "House of 1000 Manga – 10 Great Zombie Manga". *Anime News Network*. Retrieved 11 January 2014.

101. "Ring 0/Orochi's Tsuruta Directs Live-Action Film of Zombie Manga Z". *Anime News Network*. 9 April 2014. Retrieved 30 July 2014.

102. Kino, Carol (30 July 2006). "Jillian Mcdonald, Performance Artist, Forsakes Billy Bob Thornton for Zombies". *The New York Times*. Retrieved 6 May 2009.

103. "CERAP – Centre d'Etudes et de Recherches en Arts Plastiques". Cerap.univ-paris1.fr. 1 December 1994. Archived from the original on 8 March 2012. Retrieved 7 July 2012.

104. Grebey, James (3 June 2019). "How Dungeons and Dragons reimagines and customizes iconic folklore monsters". SyfyWire. Retrieved 14 January 2022.

105. Woodard, Ben (2012). *Slime Dynamics*. Winchester, Washington: Zero Books. p. 32. ISBN 978-1-78099-248-8.

106. Kay, Glenn (2008). *Zombie Movies: The Ultimate Guide*. Chicago Review Press. p. 184. ISBN 9781569766835.

107. Weedon, Paul (17 July 2017). "George A. Romero (interview)". *Paul Weedon*. Archived from the original on 20 December 2019. Retrieved 2 June 2019.

108. Diver, Mike (17 July 2017). "Gaming's Greatest, Romero-Worthy Zombies". *Vice*. Retrieved 2 June 2019.

109. Christopher T. Fong (2 December 2008). "Playing Games: Left 4 Dead". *Video game review*. Retrieved 3 December 2008.

110. "Urbandead.com". Surcentro.com. Retrieved 5 November 2013.

111. Usher, William (1 July 2012). "DayZ Helps Arma 2 Rack Up More Than 300,000 in Sales". Cinema Blend. Retrieved 3 July 2012.

112. Nutt, Christian (23 January 2015). "DayZ hits 3 million sales after 13 months in Early Access". *Gamasutra*. UBM plc. Retrieved 24 January 2015.

113. Robey, Tim. "George A Romero: Why I don't like The Walking Dead". *The Telegraph*. Archived from the original on 11 January 2022. Retrieved 13 February 2017.

114. Wexler, Laura. "Commando Performance". *The Washington Post*. Retrieved 20 April 2010.

115. Hill, Kyle (25 June 2013). "The Fungus that Reduced Humanity to The Last of Us". Scientific American. Retrieved 22 June 2018.

116. "Is the Last of Us Killer Fungus Real? – Reality Check". GameSpot-YouTube. 14 July 2013. Archived from the original on 29 October 2021. Retrieved 29 June 2018.

117. "A Discussion of Zombies and the Apocalypse in Video Games". *The Hollywood Reporter*. 27 April 2019. Retrieved 31 May 2019.

118. Barr, Matthew (17 July 2019). "Zombies, Again? A Qualitative Analysis of the Zombie Antagonist's Appeal in Game Design". *The Playful Undead and Video Games*. pp. 15–29. doi:10.4324/9781315179490-2. ISBN 9781315179490. S2CID 181693024.

119. "Preparedness 101: Zombie Apocalypse". Bt.cdc.gov. 16 May 2011. Retrieved 6 April 2012.

120. Nordstrom, David Sturt and Todd. "A U.S. Government 'Zombie' Plan?". *forbes.com*. Retrieved 12 March 2018.

121. Mogk, Matt (13 September 2011). *Everything You Ever Wanted to Know About Zombies*. Gallery Books. pp. 214–. ISBN 9781451641578.

122. Hombach, Jean-Pierre. *Michael Jackson King of PoP*. epubli. pp. 126–.

123. Dendle, Peter (2012). *Zombie Movie Encyclopedia: 2000–2010*. McFarland. pp. 256–. ISBN 9780786492886. Retrieved 19 May 2013.

124. Colley, Jenna. "Zombies haunt San Diego streets". signonsandiego.com. Retrieved 1 October 2009.

125. Kemble, Gary. "They came, they saw, they lurched". Australia: ABC. Archived from the original on 4 October 2009. Retrieved 1 October 2009.
126. Dalgetty, Greg. "The Dead Walk". *Penny Blood magazine*. Archived from the original on 6 September 2009. Retrieved 1 October 2009.
127. Horgen, Tom. "Nightlife: 'Dead' ahead". StarTribune.com. Retrieved 1 October 2009.
128. Dudiak, Zandy. "Guinness certifies record for second annual Zombie Walk". yourpenntrafford.com. Archived from the original on 23 January 2009. Retrieved 1 October 2009.
129. "Zombie Run Homepage". *Zombie Run Homepage*. Retrieved 12 March 2018.
130. Munz, Philip; Hudea, Ioan; Imad, Joe; Smith, Robert J. (2009). *When Zombies Attack!: Mathematical Modelling of an Outbreak of Zombie Infection* (PDF). Nova Science Publishers, Inc. pp. 133–150. ISBN 978-1-60741-347-9. Retrieved 9 August 2018.
131. Tchuenche, J.M.; Chiyaka, C. (14 August 2009). "Mathematical Model for Surviving a Zombie Attack". *Wired*. Condé Nast. Retrieved 9 August 2018.
132. Chodorow, Adam (7 May 2012). "Death and Taxes and Zombies". *Iowa Law Review*. 98: 1207. SSRN 2045255.
133. Mole, Beth (23 July 2012). "Zombies on the Brain: Young Neuroscientists' Popular Zombie Study Frightens Their Advisers Most of All". *The Chronicle of Higher Education*. Archived from the original on 25 February 2021. Retrieved 12 March 2022.

Photo Credits

Unless otherwise specified below, all graphics & photos were sourced from U.S. government archives and are in the public domain.

1. Pg. 9, Eucalyp / freepik.com
2. Pg. 25, Felix Koutchinski / unsplash.com
3. Pg. 27, Timothy Dykes / unsplash.com
4. Pg. 28, Bave Pictures / unsplash.com
5. Pg. 30, Nicholas Pinto / unsplash.com
6. Pg. 36, Stelio Puccinelli / unsplash.com
7. Pg. 37, pisauikan / unsplash.com